FULCRUM OF THE DOOM

NILESH MANI SINGH

We live in a fantasy world, a world of illusion. The great task in life is to find reality.

- Iris Murdoch

Contents

AUTHOR: NILESH MANI SINGH

EDITOR: RAJARSHEE BHATTACHARJEE

ILLUSTRATOR: UTKARSH YADAV

Author's Note

To my most beloved parents,

To my parents, who have always been my rock. This artistic endeavour has been propelled by your unending love, support, and faith in my dreams. My love for storytelling has been stoked by your selfless acts and steadfast support, and I am incredibly appreciative of the love and strength you have given me. This book is a tribute to the principles you taught me and the unending support that have moulded my path. I am grateful for your unwavering motivation.

To my cherished Sister,

Not only are you my sibling, but you are also my inspiration, my confidante, and my steadfast support. Our shared humour, understanding, and unwavering support have made the writing of this book an immensely important and rewarding experience. Thank you for being my rock and muse.

To Mili Di,

You were a constant source of inspiration, and reading your poems and lit a spark in me that eventually turned into a passion for storytelling. This book is proof of the deep influence you have had on my writing. Your remarks served as both a calm companion during the peaceful times of introspection and a source of motivation during the tumultuous doubt storms. It is only right that I should offer my sincere gratitude to you.I hope that when I release these pages into the world, they will resonate with the inspiration you gave and will make a lasting impression on readers, just as your words have made a lifelong impression on me.

To Cover Illustrator,

I am incredibly appreciative of Mr. Utkarsh Yadav's artistic talent and commitment, as his illustrations have brought this novel's vibrant world to life. The beautiful covers created by him really enlightened the entire feel of the novel, which also beautifully and visually captures the core of the story. It has been a great pleasure to work with such a talented illustrator, and I am indebted to him for the magic he has woven into these covers. I am grateful to Utkarsh for transforming words into images and adding even more wonderful elements to this voyage.

To my Editor,

I would especially like to express my sincere gratitude to Mr. Rajarshee Bhattacharjee, whose editorial skills have been a great help in crafting this novel. Rajarshee's astute observations, meticulous attention to detail, and resolute support have been important in moulding the manuscript into its finished shape. His dedication to quality have brought this novel to new heights. I consider myself really lucky to have had him as my editor, and I am appreciative of the joint effort we made to ensure that this book is as good as it can be.

To my friends scattered across time and place,

Friendships are the threads that weave together life's fabric, and I am lucky to have encountered amazing people at every step. I will always cherish each and every one of you, and this book is an ode to the times we shared, the jokes we had, and the friendship that helped to form who I am now. I take the spirit of these dedications with me as I release this book into the world. May the love, family, and friendship that have inspired the stories within find a home in your heart.

With heartfelt gratitude,
    Nilesh Mani Singh

FOREWORD

- The writer of fantasy has perhaps one of the most difficult jobs in all of literature: creating a world which defies the expectations of an unprepared reader, and yet keep it grounded enough to be believable. So, when about five months ago , Nilesh came up to me with the prospect of editing what would become an exercise in high fantasy, I was, by all means, petrified. We walk in the shadows of Tolkien and Sanderson, and to do so without humility is a fool's errand. And so, on a warm July evening, my work began. Sifting, cutting, and remolding as I see fit. While Nilesh had watered the plant, it was my job to trim it to a perfect bonsai. The best editors, they do say, come without sentimentality. A cold hand holding a cold scalpel, mechanically reducing a story to its best bits, at times to the author's dismay. But the editor knows best, and that's a saying which will take you far in the world of prose fiction. And I'd follow in their footsteps. I was mistaken.
- The word amateur is often seen as derogatory. And it certainly is the word I'd use to describe Nilesh as a writer. But not in the demeaning sense of the word, but rather in its rawest essence, for the word is borrowed from the Italian *amator*. A lover. In what is essentially a drop in an ocean of the fantasy canon, what you're about to read has been brought to life by a writer whose every sentence is seeped in the love for their work, and as the editor of this work, there cannot be greater praise. Trust me.
- There were moments when, I, as the primary reader let go of the scalpel and could only follow the adventures of a cast of characters whose dreams, motivations and desires kept me on the edge. Even as I corrected the occasional spelling error or the misplaced comma, I looked forward to how the journey towards a greater understanding of Doom would play out. And as I molded the final few sentences, I came upon a rather strange

feeling. I wanted more. That is a feeling which as an editor can be troublesome, but as a reader is all you can ask for.

- For an author as young, and who is but making his way into the expanse of writing, what Nilesh has to offer you is a breathtaking journey through a world which will feel familiar and oh so distant at the same time, with characters you'll come to love, and a story which will keep your hooked till you've turned the final page.
- **- Rajarshee Bhattacharjee, Book editor.**

- There are stories that resonate with us on a fundamental level, and "Fulcrum of Doom" is one such narrative. In this book, Nilesh Mani Singh presents not only a fantasy but also a richly constructed world that encourages reflection. It invites readers to embark on a journey that explores both the external landscapes of his creation and the internal landscapes of our own experiences and emotions.
- Upon reading the early pages of "Fulcrum of Doom", I was struck by the depth of insight woven into the story. It reveals aspects of life that often go unnoticed, hidden beneath the routine of our daily existence. The world Nilesh has built is filled with meaning, where every detail contributes to a larger understanding of our shared human condition. This unexpected connection compelled me to write this foreword, as I felt it was important to share these insights with others.
- Having known Nilesh for many years, I have witnessed his commitment to his craft and his pursuit of excellence. His essence permeates every page—his passion, curiosity, and introspective nature are evident throughout the narrative. He possesses a unique perspective, viewing the world through a lens that captures both its challenges and its potential. In *Fulcrum of Doom*, he has created a setting that feels both familiar and refreshingly original.
- This book transcends mere adventure; it delves into themes of humanity—how we confront our fears, desires, and inner

conflicts. It reflects on the choices that shape our identities and the journeys that lead to personal transformation. Within Nilesh's narrative, readers may find echoes of their own struggles and aspirations, prompting them to consider what it truly means to live authentically.

- While Nilesh may not openly acknowledge his achievements due to his modesty, I believe it is essential to recognize the significance of his work. *Fulcrum of Doom* provides an opportunity for introspection and offers a new perspective on familiar truths. I encourage you to explore "Fulcrum of Doom". Allow yourself to engage with this world and its story. It has the potential to evoke thoughtfulness and inspire you to reflect on your own life experiences. Nilesh has created something worthwhile here, and I am pleased to share it with you.
- Here's to your journey through this remarkable tale.
- **-Utkarsh Yadav, Book Illustrator.**

PREFACE

The world as we know it today was not always like this; in the past, magic and power were prevalent and held by a select few. The availability of means by which one could achieve immortality and something which could only be fantasized about distinguishes the present world from the one I just described. But there is one thing that never changes: the act we take to do something that interests us, something that has the potential to transform our lives and elevate us to a position from which everyone can see the blazing light, but no one wants to really make the effort to travel there. We humans have always been power-hungry and institutionalized, never desiring to be one, and constantly isolated to the point that one could only despise his own circumstance. Sadly, this will never change. It then fuels, resentment, hunger, desire, and the need to possess everything. Today, however, there is one thing that cannot ever be changed: our fate, our destiny. From the richest to the lowest, it stays the same. whatever your destiny holds. Nobody, not even you or the god, is able to stop it. Your future is in your hands. But the previous universe wasn't quite the same. There were supernatural adjustments that may reverse things. anything that should not be changed, such as fate. Even before Jesus occurred to be on the planet, there were a few lords who possessed certain mystics to oversee daily life on the planet. The god himself dispatched four lords to watch over the planet. The attributes that the lords represented were under their authoritative control. The first lord, Lord Dominicus, was the lord of redemption. He had control over this quality and the ability to either grant or take it away from a person's life. The most feared of the two lords was the Lord of Sins-Lord Carinus, who had the power to call forth all sinners and either stop or compound their sins. The lord of fate was the third lord, Lord Amandus. He had the power to alter someone's course. A king may become a beggar, but a beggar not immediately become less than an emperor. The king may even give a portion of it to a person he or she deems deserving. The fourth lord was Lord Baptiste, the lord of Karma, who oversaw people's actions and determined what should be done to them as a result. These four lords served as the earth's watchmen. This particular story, known as the epic legend of the Fulcrum of the Doom, occurred during these times. The existence of extraterrestrial forces was at its height, and the factions of imagination and fantasy abilities were not at all constrained. The division that was widespread and has persisted to the present is something that has not changed over the ages. The gap that causes the never-ending cycle of curses that a person must endure in their lifetime. Even when majestic powers sprang forth, nothing was formally established among the populace; still, there were pains and those who experienced them. The thing that baffles me the most is the fact that such were the nature of the beliefs of the people who in the first place would commit some atrocities and then go on to expect something good out of their deeds. In those times, when the concepts of fate and karma were in physical existence and people would worship them instead of gods, there were different expectations of the nature of humanity and mankind. Although the exterior of the same object changed over time, the anxieties and complications associated with it always found a way to remain relevant and to not go away, which is why it could still be seen now. But as things remain true to their nature, people and their beliefs also did. Fulcrum of the Doom is a testament of this very phenomenon, the changes come over the years and also the people were born and passed away, the pattern remains the same, but the world as we know today went through a transformation.

MAP FOR BOOK ONE

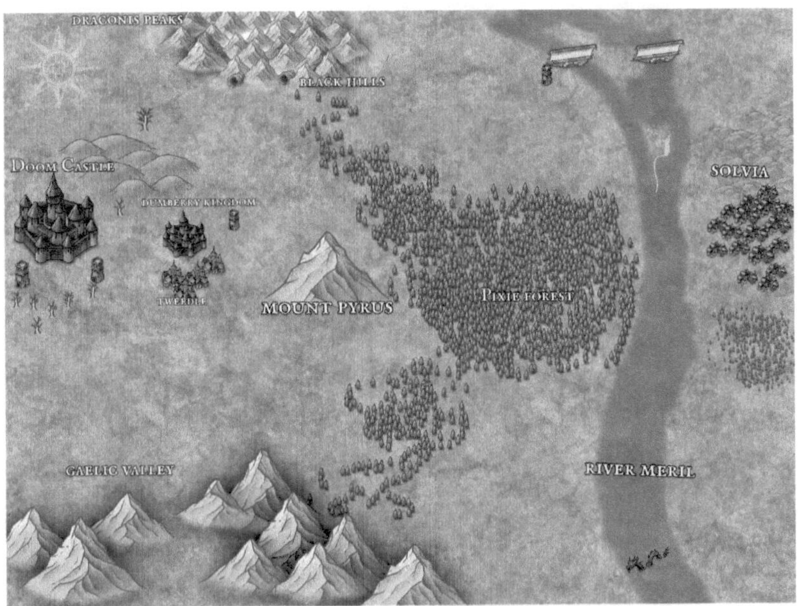

NOTE:

- The entire world of trilogy is spread across 3 books. This illustration depicts the setting where the events of book one take place. It only represents the portion of the fictional world contained in the first book.
- Throughout the book *** has been used to showcase a change of location/time.
- * or ** have been added after a section of the text to showcase exposition.

Acknowledgements

I would like to offer my heartfelt gratitude to everyone who has helped me along the way, from my family and friends to the creative individuals who shared their skills and inspiration to bring this story to life. Your encouragement and belief in my vision have been important, and my art reflects our common experiences and connections. Thank you for being an essential part of this adventure. Here are those, without whom this book would have only remained a dream.

1) Mr. Parashuram and Mrs. Sunita Singh, my beloved parents.
2) Ms. Dipti Mani, my beloved sister.
3) Late Pallavi Singh, my beloved sister.
4) Mr. Utkarsh Yadav, my talented and capable illustrator.
5) Mr. Rajarshee Bhattacharjee, my exceptional editor.
6) All of my friends who were a part of my life since childhood.

Nestled between majestic valleys and high peaks in the land of Solvia is a kingdom that has been controlled for a very long time by the enigmatic and formidable Fulcrum of Doom. An ancient being known as the Fulcrum possesses an incredible power: the power to manipulate fate itself through the antiquated art of fatumalism. For millennia, this power has moulded the fundamental fabric of existence by determining the fates of armies, kingdoms, and legendary creatures. However, not everyone feels that fate ought to be in our hands.

Fought many years ago, the Great War of Gaelic Valley was an uprising against this unnatural order. The uprising, headed by the strong warrior Magnus Leopold, who was endowed by the Lords of Creation, aimed to liberate the world from the oppressive grip of predestined destiny. Magnus felt that bravery, hard work, and free will—rather than the capricious dictates of Fatumalism—should determine a person's destiny. Even when his uprising was put down , the spirit and legend lived on, preserved in a hallowed grave atop the foggy summit of Mount Pyrus.

A new chapter has now begun.

Magnus Leopold's son Eve Leopold is raised in ignorance of his father's legacy and the weight of destiny bearing down on him. Eve is thrown into a quest that will not only uncover the truth of his heritage but also pit him against the very powers who control fate when the current Fulcrum, the feared Lord Odan, launches a vicious attack on Mt. Pyrus.

Eve's journey takes him across dangerous minotaurs, crafty werecats, and creatures from old legend that reside in the kingdom's dark regions, all of which he encounters with the support of the likes of Ceannard, Ludwig, and Murdoch. When Eve starts to piece together the details of his father's past, she learns that the way to bring an end to Lord Odan's rule is to finish a dangerous quest that Magnus once undertook in order to obtain the blessing of the four Lords who created the universe.

As a burgeoning revolt attempts to overthrow Fatumalism and the forces of evil work to maintain its dominance, the fate of the entire world is at stake. But even as Eve gets closer to his fate, there's still one unanswered question: Is it really possible for one man, bound by the legend's blood, to break free from the grip of fate and change the course of history?

The battle for Doom has only just begun, and the old stories are stirring anew, prepared to carve out a new route for Solvia, one that will be decided by the courage of those who dare to resist fate rather than by it.

I

Echoes of the Past

Evander woke up from his sleep, jumped out of bed, and started searching for the lantern. He grabbed it, lit it, and cast a quick glance out the window. He glanced at the moon after surveying his hamlet and clan and recalling the instant he made the decision to go to Doom, the place that everyone wanted to visit but only a select few could really make it there. He then softly passed by his mother and younger brother as they slept, put the lantern back where it belonged, and went to bed with the spectre of doom remaining in his thoughts. The next morning, he had trouble getting out of the bed while his younger brother Arlan was already awake and outside. Davina, his mother gave him assistance and then quickly got herself to make the breakfast. Arlan was around 17 years old, whereas Evander was around 19. Other families also lived in the little, ramshackle building where the family was housed in addition to the Leopolds. They lived in a neighbourhood called Solvia , where many families found their home back when they had nowhere else to go. There were perhaps 30 to 40 extra families residing in Solvia. While the majority of them worked in farming and agriculture, the remainder believed they would get a chance to go to Doom. Davina worked as a weaver and a market vendor of fabrics. Similar activities were also being carried out by others. The hopes that they all shared, however, were what kept them all together. They all hoped to go to doom and be free of their bad luck, their issues, and a chance to begin a new life with all of their hardships behind them.

After waking up in the morning, Evander would go check on the pixie forests on the other side of Solvia. There was a large trench between Solvia and the pixie forests. Others his age followed him this time. He had trained a horse named Nallbo, and they spent the most of their time together. Upon reaching the Solvia trench's edge, Evander surveyed it with a keen eye, as if anxious to discover something—or perhaps someone. To get to doom, one had to cross the pixie forest. Between Pixie Forest and Doom, Dumberry was located in front of Pixie Forest.

"Eve... Eve, mother's calling you!" Arlan proclaimed from behind, he came to him riding on his horse. Arlan and Evander rode back to their house together. When they arrived, Davina was waiting for them at the door and announced, "Servicemen are on their way to our community." After exchanging glances, the brothers dismounted their horses. Servicemen from Doom were the nobles working for the king of Doom, Lord Odan, famously known as the Fulcrum of the Doom. These servicemen were given the responsibility of going to nearby villages and announcing the commencement of Catharsis. The beginning of the window of opportunity to visit Doom, meet King Odan, and experience what is known as " Fatumalism " was referred to as catharsis. King Odan used fatumalist powers to alter people's fate. People who had bad luck would have a fate similar to a man who has no issues in life after being subjected to fatumalism. The miracle that was made famous in Doom was in fact a myth. For this, King Odan was well-known. He was given the ability to do fatumalism. A few people were chosen and led to the kingdom of wonders from every adjacent region of Doom. Only those residents who generated the highest income in that particular community would be chosen for that. Different people considered a wide variety of labour for this aim. And those were chosen from the same community; other communities were chosen using the same criterion. Then they would all be sent to Doom together. This had been happening from decades and people from all around who had been hardworking and lucky enough were subjected to catharsis. The residents of Solvia were jubilant about the news of beginning of catharsis, so were Evander and Arlan as they entered their home. Evander climbed up to the desk where the monthly revenue accounting register was kept. He glanced at the number, rapidly turning back the pages to compare it to the revenue from earlier months. The revenue for the current month was slightly higher than the prior totals, but Eve wasn't sure how much was enough. Arlan quickly entered the room at that exact moment.

"How much is this month's revenue, eh?" Arlan enquired.

"A little higher than in the recent months. most likely 200 more czars."

"Does that suffice?

"What do you think? The last time we had a differential of 100 czars, it did not do any good to us."

"I have heard that Ramsey is optimistic about his earnings this month."

"You can't really say who's going to make it, don't you remember Pears. People had expected him to be the last person to make it through, but he did."

Arlan nodded before leaving the room. Eve then turned towards his desk; He unlocked the bail of a dark-colored locket that he had taken out (the top of it). There were some words carved in it.

"Son, go to Doom; there you will discover your purpose."

This locket with this message by Eve's father had been with him since ages. two other lockets were with Davina and Arlan. Eve could not get a chance to really meet his father, the only close vicinity he could have with his father was having this locket. Looking at the locket brought back memories of his youth. He couldn't really recall when he first began to inquire about his father from his mother when he was a little child. Since he was little, Doom was all he had ever known or thought of. He felt some relief knowing that some of his unanswered questions would be addressed in Doom. He might even run into his father there. He wasn't precisely sure what his father intended by the message, but it had aroused Eve's curiosity sufficiently. Similar to Eve, Davina was in her room looking at the locket, which likewise had a message for her etched within "I love you, Davina! look after the family. I have gone for the purpose, that our son will carry out!!". She retracted it and remembered back to her early years and the first time she had met Magnus as she gazed down. After

turning around once more, she went to call her sons for dinner. By that time, Davina had called Eve and Arlan, and the three of them sat down to dinner as usual.

"Who told you that Ramsey had earned well this month, Arlan?"

" Charlie did, he is quite close to Ramsey and his family."

We did fairly well with our profits this month, so set that aside and let's concentrate on what we do have, Eve stated as he turned his face.

They noticed a whistling sound coming from outside as they were eating dinner. When Arlan got to his feet to seek for it, he noticed one of his pals standing nearby.

"Eh, Bendt, what's all about." Arlan shouted.

"They are dancing and feasting over at the edge near the woodlands"

Arlan regarded Davina and Eve from behind.

"Have your meal first", Davina commanded.

"Oh, mother, I'll have something better over there". After saying this, Arlan leaped out of the window and began to sprint alongside Bendt towards the feast.

"I'll finish mine, mother, don't worry", Eve remarked with a smile as he turned to face his mother. Arlan dashed over to the party where the Solvians were rejoicing about the beginning of catharsis. Men were dancing and drinking while their arms were crossed along each other. Women were dancing and singing, appearing too overjoyed at times. The young men, including Arlan and Bendt, were howling and plotting to sneak an attempt to have their hands on liquor. With a bottle of rum in his hand, Ramsey emerged from the crowd while wildly dancing to the folk music. His quick movements demonstrated his assurance in his strong chances of being chosen by the servicemen.

" Eh Ramsey, what's the matter? could you rest yourself a bit" someone asked from the crowd. By that time, Eve and Davina also had reached there. Eve joined the people dancing while Davina also sat with the other ladies who were singing. Someone from them had even brought some firecrackers, some of which had even been lighted. The sky was raised in the skyrocketing crackers. One of them rose so high in the sky that it could even be seen from the opposite side of the canyon, where the Pixie Forest begins. Near the canyon's edge, while playing, some children heard some rustling in the pixie forest. they did not pay much attention to it and continued playing. Between the canyon of Solvia and Pixie Forest, river Meril ran. It was the most prominent river across the surrounding lands, including Doom. The feast went on until after midnight, when everyone decided to leave since they were too exhausted to continue dancing and singing. After everyone had returned home around one in the morning, the pixie forest began to rustle once more. It seemed as if the forest had life of its own. Where it was coming from was still mystery, but the town didn't bother as everyone in the town was asleep. Suddenly, a grappling hook emerged from the dense of the forest and was fastened to a big boulder at the canyon's edge. The rustling of the forest increased, and then some 4-5 men wearing primitive tribal clothes with their faces being covered emerged from the pixie forest. Clinging on, they began to climb the rope as they crossed Meril and moved in the direction of Solvia. They crossed the river and came to rest on the rim of the canyon. They began to scan the area and conduct a reconnaissance. Since any error in that regard would have alerted anyone from the town, they were very careful with their moves. A few of them even ventured out onto the town's streets. One of them began searching for anyone who might still be awake and present on the streets. They discovered the booze bottles strewn throughout the canyon after some time spent scouting. They looked for any other information that would have revealed what had occurred.

"From all we could see, it appears that there was a feast."

Similar nods were made by other men. Among them said, "Thereafter, there was only a feast. We will immediately head back."

As they carefully approached the edge and fired a grappling rope from Solvia's edge to the edge of Pixie over the Meril, they all got ready to head back. They began to ascend the rope one by one while they were hanging to it to bridge the distance. One of them suggested that they send the hawk the following day after they had descended at Pixie. The Solvians awoke to the same sunny dawn the following day. People were at work, while kids were running around the streets playing. There was still one week before the servicemen arrived and announced Catharsis. The pixie rustled again, and this time a hawk came out of the dense flying high from it. The hawk flew low over the neighbourhood before landing on a person's window with a note that was crumpled and fastened in its claw. A man reached to the window, patted the bird, took the letter and opened it to read. The man read the letter, then took out his ink pen and began to write something on the flip side. He wrote " people were having a feast last night, and it will begin in a week." Then he released the hawk, allowing it to fly away and towards the Pixie. Then the man shut the window. To get to Pixie, the hawk swooped high over the Meril. One of the men in the forest raised his hand to let in land. On his right arm, the man had a menacing arrow and sword tattoo. He took the letter from its knot and started reading. Then he dashed deep into the forest. He ran across the bushes and reached a plains area where huts were built. Some tribal; native people were roaming across, while children were playing around. He then went to a much bigger hut as compared to others, and entered through the gate. there were already some people in there, and a man with a large built was sitting on the pedestal at the edge of the front of the room. The man carrying the letter formally greeted him by getting down on his one knee and lowering his head.

"Chief, the catharsis is about to begin."

When the huge man noticed him, he nodded and gestured with his hands toward some of the other men present. He was Ceannard, the leader of the Pixie combatants, the tribal warriors of the Pixie Forest. Pixie warriors have long defended the forest and the extensive secret history it holds. They have prevented anyone from gaining access to the valuable resources that are hidden in pixie. They are the ones who have long lived in and preserved the forest; their tribe is known as the Pixians. Pixians have for centuries been the tribe that has been very significant for the forest and the other surrounding localities. But for so long, they have stayed hidden from the residents of Solvians and other nearby communities. Together, isolated from the outside world, they have vigilantly guarded the forest's secrets. Ceannard peered out the window at the neighbourhood and the surrounding forest. He then squeezed his lips together and made a noise with them. Even the furthest reaches of the forest were echoed with the noise. From the side where the sound was made, a comparable sound was afterwards heard in response.

"Send another hawk explaining what needs to be done with the final confirmation tomorrow at dawn", said Ceannard. Following the uproar, some combatants ran through the forest and arrived to the Ceannard. Looking at them, Ceannard exclaimed, "It's about to begin, be prepared sons". He questioned, turning to one of them, "Where is Ludwig?"

"He must be at the river, one of them retorted. "I'll see him and inform him of the update". The contestants saluted Ceannard by bending one leg and getting to their knees, and Ceannard nodded in agreement before turning around and returning to his room. The person who had responded was Bram, who swiftly turned and made a sound akin to Ceannard in the direction of the forest's southern edge. In that direction, a loud rustling could be heard moving in Bram's direction. Suddenly, the horse's feet could be seen emerging from the bushes, but as the entire body emerged, it became clear that the upper body belonged to a human. A Centaur, it was. A being with a human-like upper body and equine-like bottom body and legs. "Murdoch, Ceannard is looking for Ludwig. He must be at the river. Call him". The mighty creature called Murdoch nodded and rushed into woods towards the river. He rustled through the woods and bushes swiftly like a wind and slowed down at the gaze of the river. He moved forward Towards the brink, and started to call Ludwig.

" Ludwig, Ceannard has called you at the hut. come fast".

The water near the brink in the river, a current started flowing towards Murdoch. A sound came out of the water as if someone was swimming up to the surface, Murdoch took a few steps back. Then with a spurt, a young man of a good built and muscular body came out of the water. He had sharp black eyes, long hairs which were tied together to his back. He was Ludwig, Ludwig Bergstorm. After taking in his surroundings, he turned to greet Murdoch, who returned the greeting.

"I'll be there, at the hut", Ludwig remarked after taking a whiff of the air and stretching. He then ran through the bushes like a breeze, heading for the dense woods. Murdoch retreated back into the other side of the river to his area. Ludwig reached at the hut and saluted Ceannard the way Pixians do. Ceannard looking at him,. said " It's about to begin Ludwig, now is the time for us to take action."

Ludwig looked at him with a glimmer of hope and then nodded.

"I will send a hawk tomorrow, stating the final confirmation."

Ceannard nodded and then resumed to look at the tribe. Next morning, Ludwig called up for his hawk by whistling, then he Attached the letters in the claw and gave it a flight. The hawk flew high with the wind, across the Meril and reached Solvia. It landed on the usual window of the building; the man was nearby the window in the room. He saw it and opened the window, took out the letter and read it. He then took out his ink pen and wrote something on it, gave it back to the bird and let it fly back. Someone called for the man from behind, "Ramsey, eh Ramsey, someone's in the shop, calling for you".

II
Beyond the Canyon

"What is it, Arlan?

Resting his arms on the counter, Arlan glanced at the owner. Beside him, Bendt looked out into the early morning street.

"Ramsey", Arlan began. "We have been thinking a lot about the Catharsis. You seem pretty confident about the outcome".

"I am pretty confident. That's not a problem now, is it?" "Yeah, we were just wondering about that. Right Bendt?" Bendt nodded.

"Is there anything else I can help you with?" "Umm, no Ramsey. We'll take your leave."

Arlan and Bendt left the shop, diverging into the growing crowd of the street.

***

The sight of a galloping horse is often a majestic sight. But through the morning market? Not so much. Through yells and raised fists, Eve rode Nallbo through the market, towards the canyon's edge. Nallbo neighed, a shrill noise, as Eve tugged on his reins. Jumping down from his horse, he patted the beast's side. Eve had been looking for ways to get over to the other

side, to the Pixie. He had this in his mind ever since that moment in his childhood. A moment so sublime, that even in distant dreams it floated in and out of his consciousness. It started as a fascination...and became an obsession.

Fluttering through the air on a moonlit sky... a fairy. She flew through the dense, barely revealing herself. She disappeared into the darkness of the forest, a spectre teasing Eve's beliefs. Eve did not also try to share this with anyone. Perhaps, it was the doubt of whether it was all a trick of the light. Or perhaps, he wanted to keep imaging her in his head, all to himself. Since then, he had come to the edge multiple times. Hoping after hope for déjà vu. But she never showed herself again. Perhaps the only way to confirm his doubt, would be to make his way to the other side.

Eve looked around. Anything, a small hope. And then, it caught his eye. A large boulder just across the brink caught his attention. He approached the boulder and stood directly behind it, observing what lay on the other side. He pondered the idea of climbing across by tying a big rope to the boulder.

Not today.

Nallbo grunted as he gently mounted him. It was time to go home.

***

Arlan and Bendt rushed through the cobblestone streets, trying to find the news of when the Servicemen would arrive.

Promises of a new tomorrow emanated through the air.

"He was a rag once, and then he went to Doom and established his own empire across the oil fields."

Ramsey, who was at his shop, got up from the counter and headed upstairs to his room.

In the distance, Eve passed the streets again, this time with a gentle gallop, carrying with him a long rope and a few hooks. The boulder awaited. Eve took hold of the rope he had brought, fastened hooks to one end of it, and then secured the other end tightly to the boulder. He then turned to face the other side to the forest, retreated a step, and dashed. Reaching the edge, he flung the rope over to the opposite side, where it snagged into a tree with two long branches. He tugged on the rope, checking if the rope was strong enough. It was. Taking a deep breath, he gently climbed the boulder and clung to the rope by fastening one hook to one end of it and his waist to the other. Below him, the Meril flowed gleefully. He felt his breath catch on in his lungs, and his vision, for a moment, blur. This was it. Looking away, he focused on the rope and continued to move across towards the other end. Slow, steady. Not a sudden move. With every bated breath, he came closer to his destination. So close, no matter how far.

THUP.

His heart threatened to escape its cage as he found himself on the other side. The fairy appeared in his mind, as he looked into the expanse of the impossibly dense forest. No time for caution...he walked into the Pixie.

***

Ahead of Pixie Forest lay the city of Dumberry, between the deep woods and Doom. Dumberry was a major financial and strategic aide to Doom, around which numerous tiny provinces with a large number of settlements had thrived, many of which provided labour for the Dumberry Kingdom. Ulrik Peerson was the king of Dumberry. His forefathers had been loyal to King Odan of Doom for all the years they had served Dumberry, and so was he. The Servicemen who were travelling from Doom to the towns would cross from Dumberry, and rest there when Catharsis would start. Among the many provinces of Dumberry, one of the most significant was Tweedle. Tweedle, among other things, boasted a lot of warrior communities. And of these, one was the Leopoldians, a significant community fighting for the nation.* Eve had entered the extremely dense back in the Pixie. He was positive that the passage he had entered was to the north courtesy of Solvia being in that direction. He proceeded to advance into the bushes, watching his surroundings as he did so. In his mind, the fairy kept floating ceaselessly. He finally arrived to a spot where the trees were typically taller than the others in the forest after a while of strolling. Eve watched, with wonder, with bated breath

And then, a rustle. Evander raise his fists, and held the rope hook in front of him. As he began to carefully scan the bushes around him, another rustle could be heard coming from the opposite side of where it had first come from. A caw, loud and shrill. And then, it appeared. An enormous hawk, through the thickets of the woods. The bird observed Eve, a cold, calculated gaze. The hawk then took off from the branch to the heights and went flying to the opposite direction. Eve let out a huff...nothing would come out of it. At least he hoped. He continued to go ahead, cutting the bushes with his knife.

The hawk, however, had other ideas. Soaring through the azure skies, it made its way home, to the Pixian tribe. She landed on Ludwig's arm, who was out in the fields. The hawk made distinctive sound, which was reiterated from Ludwig. A man of same age as that of Ludwig asked,

"What's that about"?

Ludwig looked at him and replied, "It could mean, that there's been an infiltration up north."

***

Across the city of Dumberry, at the Kingdom of Doom, Servicemen were preparing for the commencement of their journey to the nearby towns. As the news started to, spread some of the provinces of Dumberry were fast to keep up with the news. Tweedle was one of such provinces where everyone knew of the commencement the annual Catharsis. Back in the Pixie, Ludwig along with a few chosen compatriots, had started to look for the intruder. Along the way to the North, a sprinting Ludwig whistled, inviting a pack of hawks into the sky above Ludwig. He signalled something to the hawks; and the great birds went flying, ahead of Ludwig and others. Scouts of prey.

Eve was trying to rush through the forest. Doubt plagued him, and a part of him wished to return. Alas, he was in too deep. He continued running through by cutting the dense bushes. After running a while, he stopped and looked around him. The forest was all encompassing. Eve was lost.

Back in Solvia, the news about the departure of Servicemen had started to spread. People in the market started had started to talk about it. Bendt who was still at the market overheard it and rushed to Arlan.

"Arlan, Arlan! The Servicemen have departed for the journey. They could be here in 3-4 days."

Arlan raised his head from the lit pipe, and pondered, ' I need to tell this to brother". Rising up, he began to walk towards the narrow lane...and stopped.

"Where did you last see my brother" Arlan asked.

"I think he rode across the market...to the canyon's edge."

One of the men with Ludwig had gone to the edge of Pixie. He saw the rope, and the possibility of what had happened. With a shrill whistle, he signalled for the others.

"A Solvian has breached the canyon. No one has ever done that before." Ludwig's eyes wandered around the chasm.

"We need to inform this to Ceannard". A hawk floated onto his arm. Taking a leaf, Ludwig scribbled something on it with his sharp finger, and attached it to the talon of the bird, and let it fly. Amidst all this, Eve was resting under a tree. The thought of returning back had crossed his mind several times now. He was lost in the forest and now he had to find his way back to the edge of Pixie. On the other side, Arlan and Bendt arrived at the Canyon's edge and saw Nallbo there. However, Eve was nowhere to be found. Bendt then noticed the rope fastened to a boulder.

"Why in the world would he go to the forest?" Bendt asked.

"I wish I knew".

Ceannard raised his arm up. The bird sat on him, and let out of soft squeak. There had been an intrusion. The Pixian combatants raised up their arms.

"What are we supposed to do now chief?" one combatant asked. "He's a Solvian." said Ceannard.

"Do you believe the prophecy chief?" asked the combatant. "Yes, I do!" said Ceannard.

Silence took over the group.

"We'll not harm the boy in any way. If he goes back to Solvia, we'll inform Ramsey to keep his eyes on him."

Eve was still huddled beneath the tree, arms hugging himself. And then, he noticed a light. A fairy? No. A luminescent butterfly fluttering across him. Eve got up, and began to follow the butterfly to where it was headed. The dense grass led to plains. and Eve had to quicken his stride as the butterfly gathered speed. Suddenly, he saw the end of the ground over to the edge. Over to the next side of the canyon there was a large mountain full of large trees and what seemed to be strange and exotic flora. The butterfly crossed the canyon and reached to the mountain. Eve stopped at the edge. The butterfly going away instantly made him think of the fairy that he had seen in his childhood, that same luminescent wings, the same aura and the same feeling of wonder he had experienced that he experienced now. The butterfly was soon gone from his sight, leaving him to the sight of the humongous mountain he had just discovered. Behind him, the sun had begun to set. He realized he was staring at the east. Solvia is at the north of the forest. He now knew where he needed to move.

Seated among the branches, Ludwig along with his companions waited behind the bushes for anyone to come from the forest to the direction of Solvia. A hawk flew into his arm, from whose talon Ludwig retrieved a leaf. Back at the canyon's edge in Solvia, Arlan and Bendt could not reach the other side to the Pixie because the rope that was fastened to the boulder had been loosened fully and now was dispensed off and hanging by the edge of canyon. "How...will he come back now?" Bendt asked.

Arlan gave him a quick glance before mounting his steed. "You stay right here. Let me get another rope."

Bendt nodded, and Arlan went riding on his horse back to the market.

On the other side, when Ludwig set his attention back to Solvia, he could no longer see the rope. Ludwig proceeded to take out a bow he had on his back...perhaps the boy had eluded his sight. But he was wrong.

"Ludwig! There is a boy there, standing at Solvia's edge."

Eve was running through the bushes. He had spotted the Pixie's edge. He was spotted by Ludwig and other men who were hidden in the trees. While paying close attention to him, Ludwig made an effort to remain silent. Eve noticed that the rope wasn't there and began thinking of the ways to get over. Suddenly a rope was thrown at him from Solvia. He tuned up to look there and saw Arlan and Bendt holding up the rope. Then, they took the rope and fastened it to the boulder and continued to hold it tightly. Eve pulled out his hooks, fastened them to the rope, and began to move toward Solvia. Ludwig and other Pixie combatants silently watched him crossing over the mighty Meril.

Just as he landed on Solvia, Bendt hit him. "Why on earth would you go there!" Bendt asked.

"I'll tell you everything!" Eve replied, exhausted. Mounting Nallbo, the boys made way for home. Ludwig and other men climbed down from the trees.

"We must go to Mount Pyrus. Annaira's advice would be...necessary" Ludwig said.

Back in Solvia, Ramsey had received the message. He dashed up to his window and saw Eve, Arlan and Bendt coming from the Canyon's edge.

III

Infiltration and Revelation

Ceannard came out of his hut. It was Murdoch.

"I have been informed of an infiltration, chief." said Murdoch, sweat running down his face.

"Yes, there was an infiltration from the north. He was a Solvian. You along with Ludwig and a few will head to Mt. Pyrus. Annaira awaits".

Murdoch nodded, and saluted Ceannard.

To meet Murdoch, Ludwig travelled to the Pixie's southern region. Ludwig arrived and placed some flowers next to the statue of Gilmore. Murdoch came out of the trees.

They nodded at each other. No words were spoken. No words were needed.

Murdoch and Ludwig set out on their expedition to Mount Pyrus. To the east of the Pixie, where Mt. Pyrus was located, they began across the rugged southern boundaries. who was sprinting across and through the forest to the east. One had to pass through the thickest bushes in the entire forest on their journey to Mount Pyrus. Ludwig had mounted Murdoch and were supposed to journey through the forest to the east towards Mount Pyrus.

The Servicemen were on their way to Solvia by crossing the Gaelic Valley. The "Great war of Gaelic Valley" placed the Valley as an undeniable part of the history of the world, as it had shaped up the laws that currently governed the land. One of the Servicemen stopped and got off from his horse.

"Maybe, we should have a meal here. It is a straight way ahead to Solvia". Others agreed and stepped down from their horses as well.

"Hail Lord Amandus!!" the Servicemen chanted in unison.

Taking out the meals they had received in the kingdom of Dumberry, the Servicemen began to chat. One of them while having his meal started to look around and his eyes got stuck to a very large mountain that was far away to the farthest edge of the Pixie Forest. He murmured, "That's Mt. Pyrus."

"Is it true what that fellow working in administration was talking about the other day?"

"Yes, that's pretty solid, he is a man to be trusted, has worked for many years, got to know about a lot of things from him." one of them replied.

"So, there's going to be an attack on Mt. Pyrus at the end of Catharsis." "Yes, that's what the chatter has all been about."

"It was the Chieftain who had reported the matter to almighty, isn't it?"

"Yes, chieftain Gorm had spotted those aliens. That's not what Doom breeds."

"Well, I have heard that Malisons had gone to Mt. Pyrus to seek help of these aliens." "Yes, he did."

One of them got up and said, "Enough of the chatter now. We should get going."

Other nodded and got up as well. They mounted their horses, looked ahead to where they were supposed to head further and resumed their journey to the nearest edge of Solvia.

Ludwig and Murdoch were at the damp forest beyond, which was the end of Pixie. Ludwig got out of the back of Murdoch and started to examine the whole damp. He then stepped his right foot over to the damp surface to check its hardening. Quickly then, stepped back a bit and then sprinted towards Murdoch, took a jump to put his right foot on his back and then jumped towards a big tree across the land. Spreading his arms, he put his arms across the branch of the tree and started to shake it with an intend to break it. The branch snapped off and landed on the floor, Ludwig jumped from the tree in the ground, and then carried the branch. He took his knife out of his backlot and started to carve it to make it pointed. He had made it into a spear and mounted on Murdoch's back again.

"It shall work"

Murdoch sprinted through the damp with the speed of light. The damp surface had started to go beneath, and Ludwig started to push the spear on the surface and moved in a circle. The damp started to get away from them giving them a bit of time to escape.

Ludwig shouted "Faster Murdoch, faster!!!"

Murdoch screamed and got his legs out of the damp and sprinted towards the other side. As they had reached the bank of the other side, Ludwig jumped from Murdoch's back and landed on the land surface. He stretched his hands to Murdoch who leaped and caught hold of his hands, getting out of the damp. They were panting to their death and Ludwig sat under a tree. Murdoch stood up after that and turned to face the Mountain's direction. Then Ludwig followed suit and stood up.

"What do you think how far is it?" asked Murdoch.

" I think we will have to travel for the rest of the day" replied Ludwig.

r"Come, sit on my back," said Murdoch.

Ludwig looked at him and jumped on his back. Murdoch after taking a sigh of breath, began running.

In the kingdom of Dumberry, the Tenor Bureau had started to receive some highly confidential messages from Doom. The Tenor Bureau was a large building situated at the corner of the premises of Dumberry fort. This bureau was solely responsible for successfully getting the messages delivered to King Ulrik. The highly confidential messages were provided great surveillance and they were generally from Doom. This time, in order to guarantee a prompt delivery, the riders manning the bureau had departed a little earlier. Within the guarded boundary, the riders arrived at the entrance of the Dumberry fort. The riders dismounted their horses and started to tread towards the main fort hall to the king's assembly. King Ulrik was sitting on his throne listening to the daily informants of the kingdom. He was interrupted by the Chieftain who was informed of the arrival of the riders.

"My king, the riders of the Tenor Bureau have arrived for a rather urgent message, seemingly from Doom." Chieftain announced. The Chieftain was called upon by King Ulrik, who instructed him to bring the horsemen inside. In response, the chieftain permitted the riders entry. Some people were forced to leave the assembly room. Assembling in front of the king were the riders.

King Ulrik enquired, "What is the message from the Lord?"

One of the riders responded to the king after taking a breath.

"The Lord has commanded us to get ready for a full-scale attack on Mount Pyrus." Ulrik the King scowled and got up from his throne.

"I see... If so, then it is."

King Ulrik nodded and called out for the Chieftain. The riders regarded the king and returned back.

"Send word to the army to get ready for an attack soon. Also, send new artillery to replace the old ones, new commandos to begin training for an attack, and the Leopoldian army to merge with the main army."

The Chieftain stepped out of the assembly hall and instructed one of his assistants. The assistant set out on his horse to Tenor Bureau. The chieftain was a prudent man who looked at the rider going to deliver the message and thought of the impending war that could take place sooner than he had thought. He got glimpses of the "Great war of Gaelic Valley". He had seen it all, and no man who had been to war wanted to return to it. He turned his face down and began to walk back slowly. After getting the king's message, the riders set out to deliver the ultimatum to the military base. The army chief of the Dumberry military got the message of the attack that is being planned on Mt. Pyrus.

***

Davina had not talked to both of them since their arrival. She got busy making the supper, Arlan and Eve were on the terrace.

"What did you find there?"

"Nothing, just wanted to go and see what's out there." replied Eve.

"Do you even wonder about what could have happened if we had not come on time?" "I would have come out of there regardless of your help,"

Arlan turned his gaze away.

"So. it's you who will be going to Doom if we are selected tomorrow." asked Arlan. "Yes, you'll staying here with mother. I'll be away for a year." said Eve.

"I will join the Doom army, the mightiest army ever on the planet. Then with all the training and recruitment, a year would be over soon."

Arlan nodded. And sighed. Davina screamed their names for the supper. Rising up, they shouted a YES back, in unision. They got down from the terrace and sat down for the supper. Davina, still upset with them, served the plates and sat down to eat.

There was somberness on Davina's face. "Let's just have our dinner and go to bed. We need to wake up early tomorrow. Eve, just go through the accounts for the final time. And do not go to Nallbo after that. Okay?"

Following supper, Arlan assisted Davina in putting the plates back in the kitchen while Eve went upstairs to review the accounting. In order to ensure that nothing was overlooked and to prevent any potential future errors, he pulled out the account books and began to go through them, checking and matching the records as he went. He checked the accounts, placed them back on the shelf, and then sat on the balcony of the window to observe. Ramsey was watching him from the end of the lane that was directly below the window. To get a closer look at him, he began to carefully move towards the right end of the lane. Once there, he turned to face Eve.

"See you in Doom, Eve," Ramsey thought to himself.

***

Ludwig and Murdoch had reached at the edge end of the Pixie. Ludwig took out a stick from his backlot, grabbed a leaf and wrote, "Pixians seek help!". He got a hold of it and then took

a few steps back. He then sprinted towards the edge and threw it with a great scream echoing the surrounding. It landed on the edge of the mountain. Ludwig and Murdoch started to observe for something, then suddenly, from the base of the mountain, a flock of luminescent birds took to the sky, one of which soared directly for Ludwig and Murdoch. The large bird hovered above them and then landed flapping its wings.

"What is it that you seek Anaira's help for? the bird asked.

"After centuries a Solvian entered the forest of Pixie. Ceannard believes the prophecy has come to pass."

The enormous bird gave him a wary glance before nodding and said, "Hm. Perhaps."

The bird turned back and lowered his wings and said, "Hop on. And don't move too much".

Ludwig and Murdoch climbed up its back. The bird started to flap its wings and took flight. The other birds followed, as they flew over towards the peak of the mountain. As the two Pixians gazed at the horizon, they saw the most beautiful view of their life, the place where other creatures of Mt. Pyrus resided. Their luminescent lights lit up the surroundings. The other birds accompanying the one carrying Murdoch and Ludwig passed him and landed at the foot of the mountain. The fairies residing at the foot of the mountain started to pour out of their nests. One of them shouted, "Isidore, eh, Isidore."

The large bird was called Isidore, the mighty watcher of the Mt. Pyrus. Isidore flapped his wings even faster and then flew over to the edge of the mountain.

Ludwig while mounted on his back signaled Murdoch to the peak of the mountain. Isidore halted and then took a plunge higher in the air. The mountain glowed up with its luminescent personality and with the creatures living within them. With one last flap,

Isidore hovered over the top and carefully landed at the peak of the mountain. The mountain was covered in glowing trees, and the gentle flow of the waterfall painted an image of tranquility right at its edge. "Having a sincere intention and a right heart will lead you to see Anaira, who will appear in front of you," Isidore remarked as he took a step back. Then, he flapped and took a flight away. Ludwig and Murdoch were left alone on the peak in front of the glowing trees. Ludwig, taking a moment to settle himself, mounted Murdoch and they began their journey into the trees. The trees then began to light a little more and appeared to be alive. Suddenly, a creaking voice was heard across the area, someone said," They are here to see Anaira."

Ludwig and Murdoch stopped and looked around for the source of the voice. They could not see anyone apart from themselves, they continued walking to the waterfall.

"Is Anaira going to show up?" a second voice echoed from behind. Ludwig and Murdoch paused once again and surveyed the area. They couldn't figure out where the voice was coming from.

"Keep moving on, fellows; don't stop. Put an end to your search; we are the trees. You can't possibly see us, right?"

The other trees laughed in consonance with the former one and with their every giggle, their luminescence giggled too. Suddenly, amidst this a female voice came.

"Stop it at once!" the voice said. There was silence.

"I am right here, across your right." The two Pixians turned their heads in that direction and noticed a glowing tree with pink stripes. The stripes gave off a slight glimmer as she spoke.

"No one is going to bother you right now as you head to the waterfall. And keep in mind that if you declare your purpose firmly in your heart, she will show up,".

The trees dispersed to make room for them as they carefully continued walking towards the waterfall. More so than previously, trees were suddenly shining brightly. The waterfall was visible now from a distance through the dense. They came across the final row of the trees that they had to pass. The waterfall was visible now from a distance through the dense. Murdoch increased his speed looking at the waterfall. It was night but still the vicinity of the area was glowing with the luminescence of the trees. Now Ludwig dismounted Murdoch's back and started to walk along with him. They crossed the final row of the trees and saw the waterfall. A bright mist covered the waterfall and the vegetation around it, which eventually began to envelop the two of them. Murdoch attempted to get away from it, but Ludwig stopped him and told him to remain put.

"Don't run away from it; keep in mind what was said. Have a clear intention in the heart "Ludwig said.

They both maintained their stillness and shut their eyes. It moved over their bodies like an ethereal blanket, until there was nothing but the mist. Suddenly, a soft voice murmured from within the mist.

"What is it that you have come here for Pixians."

"We have come here to seek Anaira's advice and her blessings."

After a brief pause, the voice added, "I see. In that case, Anaira shall listen and come to you."

The mist glowed, blinding the two of them. Then, highly light-emitting wings that were flapping in their direction emerged from the mist . As they covered their eyes, a dazzling, sizable, and exquisitely divine fairy emerged in front of them. She was flapping her wings and stayed in the air up from the ground. Ludwig and Murdoch were flabbergasted and they knelt down

in front of her. Anaira continued to flap her wings then the flapping stopped and she stood on the ground. "What is it that the that Pixians seek help for?" asked Anaira. Ludwig looked at her and replied, "A Solvian came to the forest, in centuries. There has been a talk of a prophecy, about the Fulcrum of the Doom."

Anaira looked at him and said, "I see glimpses of the man who had come to this mountain in his final days. "

She closed her eyes and some glimpses went through her mind. She saw a dying man coming to Mt. Pyrus, he is surrounded by the fairies. Then, Anaira appeared to console him. Suddenly, Anaira opened her eyes in fury of seconds.

"I remember now, the man, Magnus was his name. He had requested a fairy to go to his son in Solvia, the fairy went in secret hiding from others and she showed herself to the boy."

Anaira closed her eyes once again, and took a deep breath. "He is going to be the next Fulcrum of the Doom."

Ludwig and Murdoch looked at each other, shocked beyond their expectations. Looking away from each other, they tried to make sense of the statement.

"Protect the boy at any cost. He shall return to where he belongs." Anaira then leaned and put her hand on the heads of both of them.

"Anaira and her blessing shall be with you". Raising her arms into the skies, she murmured 'Isidore...' before turning back and disappearing into the mist again. Isidore appeared from below the mountain and landed on front of them.

"Mount" Isidore commanded.

Ludwig and Murdoch mounted his back, Isidore flapped his wings and took a flight as the sun set to rise behind them. Isidore flew over Pyrus Mountain and through the chasm between Pyrus Forest and Pixie Forest, He took the flight to where the Pixians resided

***

It was morning and the Servicemen had entered the Solvian region. the people who had been assigned with welcoming them were awake and, they welcomed the Servicemen by beating drums and rolls and a long-standing tradition. For when the Servicement arrive, all must be present. One of them rushed to the central bell at the marketplace and started beating and ringing it to wake up the rest of the town. Hearing the sound, Eve opened his eyes and rolled out of his bed. He went to the window and looked out of it. Davina and Arlan had already woken up.

"Get ready", said Davina.

Eve and Arlan went inside to get ready followed by Davina.

At the Canyon's edge, Isidore left Ludwig and Murdoch at the bank of the Pixie River.

"Isidore would like to see you two again. Soon". Saying this he again took a flight up in the air. Ludwig and Murdoch saw him flying to Mt. Pyrus and immersing in the rays of the sun.

IV

A Kingdom Prepares

The word of the attack on Mount Pyrus had already begun to reach the general populace in the kingdom of Dumberry. A committee was established by the administrative bureau to study the issue of bolstering the army. King Ulrik had requested a meeting of the several bureaus in the Dumberry Castle. Dumberry had 4 bureaus to look upon the different matters of the state. The Tenor bureau undertook the task of communication of messages around the kingdom and beyond. The Administrative bureau handled the internal affairs of the fort and kingdom. The Defence bureau managed the affairs of the army at the borders and in case of any insurgence or immediate situation of a war. The Surveillance bureau was the final one, and its job was to investigate issues of covert espionage and associated activities. The meeting regarding the attack on Mt. Pyrus was to be held in the courtyard of

the fort where the general assembly used to be held. The Minister of Affairs was called upon by King Ulrik, upon the latter's request for a meeting.

King Ulrik stood by his throne, looking outside the window. "Hail the king".

"What is it that you want to see me about?", asked King Ulrik.

'It's about the Leopolds. They are eager to join the battle. The warriors have long waited to be on a battlefield. They are now looking for redemption from their past, from the sins of their ancestors." said the Minister.

King Ulrik turned. "Tweedle has to be protected. It has one of the most well sought group of warriors ever known to the kingdom of Dumberry."

He continued, "Only in the case of an emergency or the case wherein our army fails to capture Mt. Pyrus, shall they be called for an attack".

The Minister remained silent.

"The annual Catharsis is going to take place soon. Send a message to Doom for a unit to come and join our army."

The minister nodded at the orders, saluted the king and went back.

The information regarding the attack on Mount Pyrus was the talk of Tweedle. The area where the Leopolds lived was a bit far from where the rest of the residents lived. The residents were housed in a number of huts, and next to them was a huge field where the Leopold warriors were trained. At the time, when this news broke out, several young warriors were training. The head of the training squad was in the center hut while others were outside. A handful of Leopold youngsters could be seen coming from the other side of

the wooden fence separating them from the other Tweedle residents. To be the first to train, one of them attempted to slide through his brethren. As he attempted to cut between them to reach the front of the queue, the others cast him a suspicious glance. One of them shouted, "Hey Ebbe, hey don't cut through the line. Come back here." To this, Ebbe looked at him and smiled while running ahead through the line to the forefront. A young lad of 19 with a lean, muscular built and long hair, his eyes shined with the arrogance of youth. He stopped at the edge of the training area and looked at the trainees on the ground. He caught the instructor's attention.

"To the field. Now!"

Ebbe shrugged his shoulders and stretched his body before entering the field. Out of the trainers training there, a tall, well-built warrior walked out, and stood next to him. Ebbe stared right into his eyes and gave his fist a knuckle. The instructor pointed to the ropes fastened to the tall wooden shackles and stated, "One who pins the other down on the ground wins this and gets a chance to go to practice over the ropes there. Are we clear?"

"Crystal", the young man whispered. After glancing at the ropes, Ebbe turned to face his opponents

After glancing at the ropes, Ebbe turned to face his opponents. He sped up and charged towards him, aiming for his torso.
***

Back in Solvia, all gathered around the Servicemen who were about to announce the annual results. Eve, Arlan and Davina were standing in the crowd which was eagerly waiting for them to announce the results. The Servicemen stood on a podium, while one of them opened the ceremonial scroll. Ramsey came down from his shop to join the commotion. Eve

looked at him and gave him a glance. He glanced back. He knew who had been to the other side.

One of the Servicemen started speaking.

"Solvians, we are here to announce the annual result of the Catharsis for your province. We will be selecting the three of the most income-generating members of the families."

Cheering ensued, and the Servicemen had to calm them down.

"The families which have been selected for the annual Catharsis are the Luisons, Ramsey...and Leopolds."

Upon hearing this, the crowd cheered up while hugging those who were selected.Eve, Arlan and Davina stood there in silence looking at each other. They had tears in their eyes. Davina hugged her two boys while smiling erratically. Destiny.

The Servicemen congratulated the chosen individuals and announced that they would be departing for Doom the following day. Accommodations were made for the royal messengers. They were to stay at the village's central hut, which is where they could see the Canyon's Edge just around the corner. A few locals approached the stage and motioned with folded hands for the

Servicemen to leave so they could be led to where they would be staying. People were busy congratulating the chosen ones, while Ramsey quickly left the crowd and climbed up to his shop terrace. He opened a closet, took out a paper and an ink pen and started writing down something. He whistled looking outside his window, the same hawk descended down to him. Tying the letter down on its talon, he let the hawk fly. Arlan, Eve, and Davina returned to their house. Eve was grinning as they made their way back to their house, and Davina caught her eye. Arlan looked at Eve.

"You are leaving tomorrow, Eve, tomorrow is the day finally for you."

Eve looked back at him and replied, "I'll be back soon Arlan, you need to stay here and look after mother and this place."

We need to pack your things first, Davina stated as she intervened. Eve nodded before rushing upstairs to his room and saying, "I'll be back." He entered his room, began gathering his possessions, opened his desk, took the locket out, held it between his palms, and peered out the window at the length of the Pixie Forest.

The Servicemen were made to reside in the village's main hut. For the trip to the Doom the following day, their horses were being fed at the neighboring stable. Apart from the horses of the Servicemen, three extra horses were also present there at the stable provided by the Solvians. The chosen ones for the Catharsis were called at the central hall for them to attend a ritual which was held every year before the chosen ones departed for the Catharsis. The chief of Solvia was present there to meet the chosen ones for the last time before they left for Catharsis. When the packing was complete, Eve, Davina, and Arlan left their house. Davina saw the happiness of the Solvians as they gazed upon Eve. The neighbours arrived and struck up a conversation with her. Ramsey too had come out of his shop. Eve looked at the other corner of the street and saw Oliver Luison too coming out of his hut. Families of all the three met at the junction of the street. Ramsey came to Eve and hugged him.

"You worked really hard. I saw you brothers and your mother working very hard."

Eve smiled. "I know you are only one left of your family, certainly you made them proud today."

Oliver also joined them as they awaited the last call from the Central Hall with their families. At the podium of the centre hall, the village chief lit the torch and bowed his head in prayer.

He then left the podium and walked over to a massive mirror. He displayed the torch in front of the mirror. The central hall was fully illuminated once the mirror magnified the torch's light ten times. The families who had been waiting for the signal at the door saw it, and slowly moved towards the hall. They entered the hall through the main gate and saw the village chief walking towards them. He was carrying the lit torch in his hand as they approached them.

" The ones who will be going for the Catharsis shall step forward." Eve, Ramsey and Oliver stepped out.

The torch was brought closer to them by the village chief. The Village Chief instructed the group of three to touch the torch and close their eyes.

This was it.

Eve, Ramsey and Oliver gasped as they touched the warmth of the torch. A magnificent vision engulfed their minds, a vision of everyone who had visited Doom seeking Catharsis; some were crying so much they were on their knees while others were laughing wildly. All three gasped. Eve noticed a man in particular. He was grinning while gazing distantly at Eve. Then the vision changed to show the man sprinting towards a tall, strong man brandishing a sword. Suddenly, the man in motion with the sword turned to Eve and yelled his name.

"Goooooo to Doooom," the man yelled.

Eve opened his eyes, after getting scared. A single tear rolled down his cheek. He looked at the other two, who had opened their eyes too, visibly shaken by the vision. The village chief then took the torch away from them and in a baritone, said, "Each of you must have heard some kind of voice reaching out to you. Keep that within yourselves. Our ancestors who got a chance to get to

Doom had a voice of their own and these are their voices. Don't let your guard down. For Solvia's sake."

Eve was startled at this instance, he turned back along with others to get back to his home. The village chief put the torch again on the podium and bowed before it.

***

Back in Tweedle, Ebbe sat on the dusty ground, rubbing his knuckles. The man he was fighting against was sat beside him, blood dripping from his nose. One of Ebbe's comrades walked to him

"You were very impressive today Ebbe. The army would be more than glad to pick you up"

Ebbe's ears perked up and he looked at his friend. He stood up and asked that boy again about what he knew. His friend replied, "An attack has been planned and for that, they will be recruiting to strengthen the army."

Ebbe smiled to this and placed his hand on the shoulder of his friend. suddenly, some of his other friends called him as they were returning back to their area the other side of the fence. Ebbe hugged his friend and headed towards his friends. He was walking away when the training chief approached him.

"You were outstanding in the training today. Starting tomorrow, you will be the first ones to train."

Ebbe smiled. "I will not disappoint you, sir."

Ebbe ran his fingers over his knuckles, as his friends passed through the fence one by one, leaving Ebbe behind. He observed all the Malisons living in their filthy homes and pitiful conditions as he stepped onto the other side. Malisons were Tweedle residents who opposed King Odan during the Great Rebellion. As a result, they were taken from Tweedle's normal population and forced to reside on the other side of the fence. Malisons lived in deplorable conditions, subject to the whims of the other Tweedle residents. For a limited time, children and teenagers were permitted to cross the fence to the opposite side, as the other side of the fence had all the parks, market and the training area, and as the sun began to set, all the Malisons had to return back to their huts in a queue. Ebbe's smile vanished from his face, as he started to descend towards his hut. His friends wished him goodbye and went to their huts. Ebbe continued to tread onto the way by brushing away the bushes with his hands. His hut was at the center of the grand bushes. He entered his hut. His family was waiting for him over the dinner.

"How was the training today?" his father asked.

"The best for me", Ebbe replied. He then sat down on the ground and said," They are recruiting for the army."

His mother smiled and said, "That's so great to hear, but then would we be allowed to live on the other side?"

"Well, I am not entirely sure but once you get into the army, you do get a lot of respect." his dad replied.

"I'll get into the army. I don't care how. I'll get into it." said Ebbe. His mother put the banana leaf in front of him and began to serve the food. That day they were lucky enough to get some gravy of fresh bushes. Ebbe's family had never had bread for ages. Ebbe's wish to have the luxury to have a bread for food had been with him for so long. His parents had grown so weak and timid over the years, that they appeared paper thin. Following dinner, Ebbe and his family retired to sleep on some giant leaves they had collected from the forest. Ebbe's parents had gone to sleep, he sneaked out of his leaf-bed and went out of the hut. He went through to the bushes; he ran through the large bushes to the other side of where they lived. He reached the outer skirts of Tweedle from where provinces of Dumberry ended. He tried to see to the stretches

beyond Dumberry. He had longed to seek the discovery of what lied beyond Dumberry. Climbing a tree at the corner, he rested on the branch and looked at the frontiers beyond Dumberry. He had never left Tweedle. He had not only dreamt of going to Dumberry, but even to the beyond of this kingdom. A dream that was close to his grasp. His waking dreams led to sleep, and he dozed off on the branch.

Next morning, it was time for the chosen ones to depart to Doom. The Servicemen had been awake since early morning and were practicing yoga. Eve had already awoken. The entirety of Solvia had come out of their houses, marvelling at how the way to the exit of the village had been decorated. The Servicemen came out the central hut on their horses to the way to exit. The village chief ambled towards their direction with all the chosen ones and their families. Eve, Ramsey and Oliver climbed onto the horses and began to tread to the Servicemen. They joined Servicemen who were waiting for them, and greeted them. Solvians were all there at the way to the exit and were cheering for the chosen ones as they began their journey for the Catharsis

Eve dismounted his horse as Davina and Arlan emerged out of the crowd. Davina hugged Eve with tears in her eyes as Arlan joined in.

"I will do the best I can and meet the Fulcrum of the Doom. Arlan, you need to take care of Maa and yourself till I get back. Train regularly and wait for my letters. Okay?" Arlan nodded. Davina nodded. Eve nodded.

The Servicemen then signalled the chosen ones to prepare for departure. One of the Servicemen took out an arrow and shot it up in the sky. The arrow went up and then blasted in flares. It had begun. Eve smiled and looked back at Davina and Arlan who smiled back at him.

V
Gathering Forces

While Murdoch had been meditating in the deep forests of Pixie, Ludwig was in the centre of the woods, with other Pixie combatants and centaurs. Suddenly a young centaur came running towards Murdoch, panting and sweating profusely. Murdoch opened his eyes. "What is it?"

The young centaur replied, "We were out there towards Mt. Pyrus and I saw the footprints of...of a Minotaur."

Murdoch gripped him by his shoulders while getting up from where he was sitting and widening his eyes.

"A Minotaur? They haven't been around in decades. Are you certain that those footprints were of a Minotaur?"

The young centaur nodded. Murdoch looked around in disbelief, and commanded the young Centaur to return to the others. Murdoch then ran in the direction of where the Minotaur had been spotted close to Mount Pyrus. Sprinting across the forest through the bushes and streams along the way, he stopped by the area from where the end of the Pixie Forest started. He started looking for the footprints as had been mentioned to him. He was removing leaves off the ground and then his eyes matched with the large footprint, he got close to it and examined it. And then, it caught his attention. A significantly large footprint. He whistled in a shrilling voice thrice onto the forest. A group of hyenas came running towards him and behind them was a wild dog. The wild dog came near Murdoch. He lifted his hoof up, and the dog seemed to nod. It sniffed the footprint, and its ears perked up as it began to move in the direction of Pixie to the north-west. While the hyenas were in his rear, Murdoch followed it. The dog stopped at the edge of the Pixie Forest, with Gaelic valley on the other side. Murdoch looked at that direction before turning to pat the dog, and the wild beasts returned back to the woods.

Murdoch looked around the area, and stomped over the ground to check for any other signs of infiltration. He then looked at Mt. Pyrus from that distance. All in due time.

Murdoch made the decision to head back to the Pixie combatants' base camp. On his way to the base camp, he dashed through the bushes, chopping anything in his path. The resident in the base camp of Pixie combatants were doing their chores when they heard Murdoch coming towards them running. He stopped at the main hut and asked the guard about Ceannard. By then, even Ludwig had come out of his hut to Murdoch.

"What is it?", asked Ludwig.

"We should go inside and talk about it, Ludwig".

Both of them entered the main hut and closed the doors. Ceannard was sitting on a pedestal along with the walls and meditating. Ceannard sensed them and opened his eyes. He came down from the sitting pedestal

"Tell me"

Murdoch replied, " A Minotaur has infiltrated within the boundaries of Pixie Forest. Upon hearing this, Ceannard's eyes shot up.

Ludwig began, "But it has been so long since a Minotaur had entered our forest." "The young ones spotted it first near Mt. Pyrus. I checked. They're right".

"Near Mt. Pyrus? That is not good, not good at all. I do not feel right about it, there should not have been an infiltration there. We need to send some combatants t here, immediately" said Ceannard.

He then moved out of the hut through the main hut, seeing him the combatants training stood in attention. All the combatants stood in order in front of Ceannard, who was at lodge of the main hut above the ground.

"An infiltration has been reported, a grievous one near our sacred place, Mt. Pyrus and that too by an age-old enemy. A Minotaur. We do not know why one of them infiltrated our lands after ages but whatever they are up to, it is our duty to stop them. And we will. Pixie Combatants will not let anyone, any evil force to come near to our place of worship. From now on a troop of combatants will guard the area nearing the Mt. Pyrus, and the shifts will change every night."

The combatants saluted Ceannard as he went inside his hut, Murdoch and Ludwig following him. A troop of combatants went inside their huts to get their weapons. Other Pixians had started to come out of their huts to see the commotion. The troop was headed towards the area of Mt. Pyrus. Ludwig and Murdoch were the ones watching over the troop.

***

Back in Dumberry, it was the day for the inspection of artilleries and training of the youngsters who were about to join the military. Chieftain Gorm was in his dorm watching all over the artilleries being taken away on the horses from his window. Walking out of the dorm, he made it towards his steed and ordered for his horse. Climbing his horse, he rode through the exit from the fort to the training area. The trainees were training in the area to join the military for the upcoming attack on Mt. Pyrus. He came over to the spot to keep an eye on the training. Ebbe huffed as he practiced ground assaults; Gorm observed him finish off his opponent with a slick attack. He called the trainer from the training area, who came running to him. He saluted the Chieftain.

"Who is that trainee who just performed the ground assault?" The Trainer replied. "He is Ebbe. A Malison."

Gorm looked at him and then at the boy.

"The Malisons are to be included in the military and they would be sent for the initial attacks as you mentioned. But this boy has got exemplary fighting skills."

Gorm looked back at Ebbe, as the instructor continued talking about him. Ebbe then moved away from the field and went to drink water from the river nearby and across the training field.

Nodding, he mounted his horse and rode towards the bureaus. Gorm entered the Tenor Bureau as he was expecting some update on the chosen ones and how far they have reached from their villages. One of the messengers at the Tenor Bureau had been called off by the message received by the Servicemen, he then moved all the way to where Gorm was. Gorm was about to call for a messenger as the said messenger came down to him. He saluted Gorm, who saluted back to him.

"They will be here tomorrow morning Chieftain. All the arrangements regarding their initial stay have been made."

"Good, the ones joining the department of defence should be deployed to the Defence Bureau in a matter of days for the preparation of the attack. The best ones, the fastest, the ones who are the most brutal are the kinds we are looking for. King Ulrik is very clear regarding the kind of troops we will be sending for the initial attacks at the Mt. Pyrus. He will be addressing the Defence bureau soon, take care of these things." Said Gorm.

***

The Servicemen along with the chosen ones had reached the bypass route to Dumberry which was along the way of Gaelic Valley. They had stopped to have some food and decided to continue journey the next day. Eve along with the other chosen ones had come down from their horses while the Servicemen had lit up some bonfires nearby where they were preparing for some food. The Valley was glowing in the night, as the northern stars were just above the valley that night. Ramsey went a bit far from the commotion and lit up his cigar. Oliver went to Ramsey and asked for a puff from his cigar.

"This place right here holds so much importance for us, even for the people in Doom." said Ramsey.

"You're talking about the great war of Gaelic Valley. I have heard a lot about the war in my family", said Oliver.

Ramsey continued as he turned to look at Eve, "The loom of the impending Doom lies before us. Unusual circumstances will force us to find a way out".

The annual fatumalism for that year was to take place in a week at Doom. The Servicemen passed on this knowledge to the chosen ones, and after having dinner by the bay of the Gaelic Valley, they all started to set up their camps for the night.

***

The dens of the minotaurs were located far to the southwest of Pixie forest. These dens housed a population of minotaurs, who were ruled by Vagallath, the Minotaurian king, who dwelt at the top of them at the base of the black hill. The Black hill was the entrance to Draconis Peak, the realm of the world where dragons lived and ruled. The last time the dragons of the Draconis peak gave force to their wings was during the great war of Gaelic Valley, and they had been calm and dormant for a very long time. Since the time of inception of the world, certain creatures were blessed by the four lords of the world. These creatures later evolved into dragons after getting divine abilities from the blessings. The role of the world's most powerful creatures, the magnificent dragons, was to give their wings strength and to step in when mankind were about to demand their eradication. Many attempts had been made by many kings and warriors to enter Draconis peaks and try to convince the mighty dragons into helping them by fighting for them in a battle. But as soon as someone tried to cross the Black Hill by fighting off the minotaurs, the Dragons' guards finished them off. Draconis Peak had the spell by all four lords to weed out those who came with selfish motives, only those with pure energy could pass through the spell without getting hurt by the dragon guards.

*

At the bay of the Gaelic Valley, Servicemen and the chosen ones had finished their dinner. They started to wrap all the things for their departure. All of them sat on their horses and began the last stretch to Doom.The Servicemen decided to travel in night because of the prospects of reaching the kingdom in the morning itself. Off they went on the path to Doom on their horses leaving behind the Gaelic Valley.

In the Black Hill, the minotaur who went to Pixie Forest had just returned. Vagallath was inside his cave, praying to the lords of Draconis Peak. He opened his big, brooding eyes when he detected the arrival of one of his kind. In response to the approaching minotaur, he snarled. The sound of Vagallath's snarl caused his kin to emerge from their caves as well.

The minotaur entered the cave. At seeing his king, he nodded, and let out a snarl. This was the sign of the successful infiltration that he had done in the Pixie Forest. Vagallath was the only minotaur among all of them who could talk, one of the many blessings he had got from the lords of Draconis Peak. He walked up to the big boulder, almost like a pedestal, and declared, "WE WILL ATTACK, SHRED AND ANNIHILATE MT. PYRUS AT THE INSTRUCTION OF LORD ODAN, THE FULCRUM OF THE DOOM!"

The other minotaurs rejoiced when Vagallath exclaimed this by snarling aggressively and frantically.

***

In the province of Tweedle, among several huts and other stay-outs resided the Leopoldian community. They were the descendants of the great warriors of Leopolds. They were the ones who were available for any kind battle or even an assault attack on other kingdoms. The potential attack on Mt. Pyrus was in the minds of Leopoldians, who were about to start to the preparations for the attack. Back from the huts of the Leopoldians, was the way to woods where Ebbe lived in his hut. It was around midnight when Ebbe sneakily came out of the bushes of the woods back to the place of the initial residency of Tweedle. He watched his steps as he crossed the huts, and stopped at the corner most hut. He looked around and whistled a slow shrieking noise into the window of the hut. He tried to sneak into the window, while again whistling, this time a bit gently. A soft voice came from inside the room through the window.

"Stop it now! Just...a moment"

Ebbe smiled and stopped whistling. And then, the windows opened. A young woman in her late teens put her foot outside the window while holding onto the lashes on the side. Ebbe helped her by holding her hands and pulled her out. A soft breeze washed over her, making her pretty hair sway. She leaned forward to hug him as he grabbed her by her waist, then slowly swirling his hands over her cheeks. She held him by his waist, and pushed herself onto his torso.

"We should go to the woods, Elsa" said Ebbe as he hugged her. The young girl nodded.

Elsa held Ebbe's palm, as they slowly walked towards the woods. "How's your training going on, Ebbe?"

"It's fine, I hope to join the squad soon." "You will, really soon," said Elsa.

Ebbe smiled at her and lifted her on his arms. He took her into the more remote areas of the forest. Ebbe peered up at the tree as they came to a stop beneath it. They embraced by hugging, and smiledwhile staring into each other's eyes. Ebbe soon undid the robe of her backless dress and took it off. He took her in his arms again and shook the branch over them, leaves showered on them.

. Above them, the winds shook the leaves as well, falling onto them like tropical snow.

They laid on the ground naked, as Ebbe caressed her.

"I will have to stay inside the Doom fort for the completion of training and eventual selection into the corps." Said Ebbe.

Elsa held his hands tightly and kissed him. "Try to come and meet me once in a while."

"I will... But I will have to be disciplined in order to get to the high ranks. I need to get my parents out of that hut, provide them with a decent living. Being a Malison, it has always been such a struggle. I will...have to be the best.".

Elsa saw the determination in his eyes. Ebbe moved a bit and fetched their clothes. He handed it over to Elsa and took what was his.

"We should head back."

As the run began to climb up its ranks, both of them ran back to Tweedle.

Both of them ran back to Tweedle as the sun was about to rise. As they reached the Doom fort, Eve, along with others and Servicemen, had just crossed through Tweedle. Ebbe and Elsa were moving cautiously through the underbrush when they noticed the Servicemen passing by the Leopoldians' huts. Eve was looking around like a child, eager to see anything alike that he had seen before. Ebbe caught the gaze of Eve who was just crossing, the path leading up to the bushes and woods. For a moment, their eyes met. A silence followed.

Eve looked away as Ebbe and Elsa escaped through the other way leading up to the huts.

***

Eve and others crossed Tweedle. Along with them, other chosen ones joined them as well as they formed a unison. the grand entrance of Doom fort was in front of them as the unison approached. The grand gate of the Doom fort opened as the chosen ones finally arrived at Doom. Eve smiled as he crossed to enter the entrance into the territory of Doom. Eve jumped off his horse to see how the Doom is like. the servicemen went ahead of them to make them stand in unison. Eve, Ramsey and Oliver stood together among the unison as the grand gate of the Doom fort closed behind them.

VI

Chosen Paths, Divided Loyalties

The chosen ones travelled through the main gate into the barracks where they were supposed to stay. They eagerly looked all around them, the place where they always wanted to be, is where they were now. There were big posters on the walls in the street stating about the catharsis. The vendors in the street looked at the chosen ones as they made their way through the streets to the barracks. They had to slog through the lengthy lines in front of the barrack.The Servicemen cleared the way for Chieftain Soren, Head of Administration. Soren was flanked by soldiers as he rode his cart of horses. When he emerged from the cartel section where he was sitting, the chosen ones caught a glimpse of him. He was saluted by Servicemen, and the chosen ones followed suit. Soren marched ahead of the chosen ones while maintaining his composure. "You, all of you are the ones who have showed their devotion and hard work towards this kingdom through your work, the amount of revenues you all have produced has been exponential for the kingdom. Now is the time for all of you to prove your loyalty to the one and only, the FULCRUM OF THE DOOM. Whatever department is being assigned to you, work tirelessly to prove your worth and be a part of the Catharsis." He then turned around and exclaimed," Let the annual Catharsis begin!" The whole city roared in unison. The chosen ones rejoiced and clapped as well with the others. With some sparkling flames in the air, the chosen ones departed for the

barracks. Eve looked around the people and place while Ramsey walked up to him and asked," You have been up to join the military corps, Eve?"

Eve smiled.

"Yes, military corps is where I would like to work. Ramsey what is it that you will be working for in here?"

Ramsey looked around and then turned to him and replied, " Military corps". Eve opened his eyes wide open due to shock.

"Ramsey, you had a shop in Solvia, how come you're willing to join the military corps."

"I have heard that military soldiers are prone to move higher in the hierarchy of the ones in Fatumalism", replied Ramsey.

"But is it worth risking your life?"

Ramsey turned, looked at him, "Then why are you risking your life, Evander." Evander was stunned, as he did not have the answer for that.

"I shall figure that out too."

He continued walking with others towards the interiors of the entrance of the barracks. The entrance to the barracks were very huge and as the chosen ones stood in front of them, the Servicemen approached the entrance first.

A loud siren blared the atmosphere and the grand entrance to the barracks opened. The chosen ones looked inside the barracks, and the Servicemen announced, " PROCEED!!". They started walking inside as the Servicemen followed. The barracks had large sections of rooms inside. At the middle of the barrack, there was a large dining space for all the chosen

ones. While at the edge of each section were guards at duty. The chosen ones then made their way to the various rooms.

***

Some of the Pixie combatants were manning the border of the forest where Mount Pyrus was. Ludwig had been near Murdoch's hut at that very moment. Ludwig was sitting in meditation, his hands folded. He sensed something in the bushes behind him all of a sudden. He opened his eyes and quickly turned to see what it was. He leapt up and into a standing stance. After giving the bushes a quick glance, he hurried over to them and peered inside. Something dashed across the edge of the bushes from his behind; he turned to check but it had escaped by then. Ludwig set his eyes and sprinted in that direction. He sprinted through the area of the huts to the edge of the forest to the other side. He then stopped and looked around. Silence...and then a blow of wind. And with the wind, a blow right to his face. Ludwig retreated back, and realised the stature of his adversary. A Werecat. Half cats and half humans, Werecat's boasted the speed of the former and the intelligence of the latter. The Werecat growled ferociously and took its long claws out. Ludwig jumped to his feet and took a defensive position as the werecat charged at him with sharp claws. Ludwig bowed slightly to aim for the werecat's legs, but the werecat outsmarted him and kicked him with its legs. Ludwig fell to the ground, kissing the dust.

Now that it was in charge, the Werecat began to circle Ludwig. Ludwig enquired, "What is it that you want?"

Another growl from the Werecat.

"The Pixians, each and every member of your tribe—men, women, and children. You shouldn't be living well here after driving our species away. We were a part of this forest too; the Pixie belonged to our species just as much as it does to your tribe."

"You were never a member of this forest; stop thinking of yourself as a Pixian!" Ludwig stated as he turned to face him. "You didn't care about other species; all you did was hunt."

"That is how forests are intended to be. The survival of the fittest." The Werecat swayed its tail, almost mocking Ludwig.

"That's not how Pixie is, and that's not how our forefathers, the Pegasus' were" Ludwig stood up and faced the feline.

The werecat prepared to receive his strike and attack him as he charged at him. As soon as he got near the werecat Ludwig got into his lap and slid right through between the legs of the werecat. He got up, turned around grabbed his head and smashed it onto the ground. The werecat was on the ground when Ludwig grabbed his tail and started to twist it, the werecat started to scream in pain. To signal the nearest Combatants, Ludwig whistled. The Werecat made an attempt to escape, but Ludwig began to twist its tail even more tightly. When the whistle blew, some of the combatants ran there. They placed the werecat on the ground after tying it up with a rope.

"Take him to the Chief", Ludwig commanded. "And make him talk."

The Combatants picked it up and started to dragged it to Ceannard following Ludwig, who assumed the lead. At the other corner of the edge nearby Mt. Pyrus, Murdoch was patrolling the area with other combatants. Murdoch turned to face the combatant and then left to see the Werecat at the Chief's hut. He leaped from his spot and began to run in the direction of the Chief's hut. The combatants carried it and brought it in front of Ceannard who was waiting for it to come.

***

"A Werecat in our forest. What is it for that you entered the Pixie." asked Ceannard.

The Werecat growled and laughed a bit while trying to move across and near Ceannard, while the combatants put their spears forward and surrounded it. The Werecat stopped to go any further.

Ceannard moved forward towards him, held his face and lifted it.

"This forest is done for. Your tribe, children, women, everyone. You are all doomed."

"What is it that you mean?" asked Ceannard. He made a gesture to a combatant who then put his foot on the tail and started to crush it. The Werecat screamed in pain.

"Tell me. Now" said Ceannard.

"ATTACK! There is going to be a full-blown attack!" said the Werecat aggressively, pointing at the direction of Mt. Pyrus. Ceannard turned to look at the direction of his finger.

"Mt...Pyrus?" asked Ceannard with a trembling voice.

"Yes, and this forest too will be destroyed and then your tribe will have to leave as well like we did." said Werecat.

Ceannard took a step backward in shock while looking at the direction of Mt. Pyrus. His eyes floated as he looked around him at his tribe, at his people.

"Who, who is it?" Ceannard asked ferociously.

"Fulcrum of the Doom, Lord Odan" replied the Werecat.

Ceannard was so horrified by it that he could not believe it. He had never anticipated that the Fulcrum of the Doom would attack Mt. Pyrus in such a manner, a full-blown attack.

Ceannard kneeled next to the beast. "We had a minotaur infiltration a while at the plains near Mt. Pyrus. What was it about. This...attack. Are they related?"

The Werecat said, "Minotaurs will be assisting the forces in the attack at Mt. Pyrus," looking directly into his eyes.

Now that Ceannard was beginning to make sense of everything. Ludwig and Murdoch had stopped at the location of the Werecat when they eventually made it there as well. Ceannard looked at them with a fear in his eyes. They had also sensed the eerie feeling that had engulfed the entire surrounding.

"An attack, a full-blown attack on Mt. Pyrus has been planned by the Fulcrum of the Doom." There was silence.

"The werecats and minotaurs are going to be a part of the attack. You both need to inform Isidore about the attack and send a message to Ramsey about it", said Ceannard. He continued, turning to face the Werecat, "Take him to the huts and hold him captive."

The combatants dispersed and took the werecat away to the captivity hut in the main area. Ludwig turned around and whistled vigorously looking at the sky. From the sky, a hawk descended and perched on his arm. Ludwig stroked it. Murdoch was continuously surveying the entire area, scanning every crevice, and sniffing the air for any strange odours. After making sure that there was nothing suspicious or anything to worry about, the three of them descended towards the main huts area.

"There should be no word of the attack among the families and we need to start evacuating them out of the main huts area to a safer place." said Ceannard.

" The Centaurs must be of great help in this concern. we shall carry all of them to a safer place." said Murdoch.

Ceannard nodded indicating his approval. The three of them reached the main huts area. Ludwig plucked a leaf of a tree and inscribed "ATTACK ON MT. PYRUS, PROTECT THE BOY", and fixed it with the talon of the hawk. The hawk then fluttered its wings and took the flight up in the sky. Murdoch suddenly thought of his family, he saluted Ceannard, and solemnly began," I need to take your leave chief. I must see my family now."

Ceannard nodded.

The children of Centaurs were playing outside the huts while the female centaurs busied themselves with the domestic. Some were galloping to the forest for firewood. Murdoch went straight up to the statue of their Pegasus leader, Agnar, who fought in the great battle

of Gaelic valley. He prostrated himself in front of the statue and offered flowers as an act of worship. Velda, his wife, emerged from the woods and noticed Murdoch standing in front of them. While the other female Centaurs moved to the other side, she quickened her pace and headed towards him.

When he noticed her approaching, Murdoch instantly turned to face her. Velda enquired, "I thought you had gone for the patrolling."

"I had Velda, but I need to tell something very important to you." Murdoch replied.

He took her to their hut and shut the door. Velda looked tensed as she put the basket that she had been carrying on the table, and came close to Murdoch.

"What is it Murdoch, I can see it in your eyes" Velda replied.

"We need to evacuate this area Velda along with the women and children of the Pixians." "Why? What...what's wrong?"

There was terror in Murdoch's eyes.

"Chief will be addressing us soon. Till then... just get the things together." Velda hugged him he caressed her. He then bent a little to kiss her belly. "A warrior child of a warrior father."

He then held her hand and exited the hut. Velda, holding her belly, looked around for other Centaurs.

***

The chosen ones had been given their separate rooms to stay. They were going to be assigned the work department the following day. Eve was in his room looking out of the window, thinking of Davina and Arlan. Ramsey was in his room just across the lobby. He was writing about how the day went, as he had been documenting everything. He looked outside the window at the moon. There was silence. But not for long. He heard a sound he was all too familiar with. He stood up and saw a hawk approaching him towards the window.

The hawk fanned its wings in the air before diving directly the window. Ramsey got hold of the hawk and caressed it, thinking about what could be the message for him at that hour. He took out the leaf attached to its talon and unfolded it. His eyes opened wide and a few back steps were taken by him. The sheer horror of the message engulfed him. 'Attack'. He looked at the hawk, stretched his hands out and caressed it before let it out into the skies. He never imagined that the ultimate revelation had to be made this early to Eve. He sat down on his bed and turned the pages of his diary. He wrote down the date of that day, and began writing on the page after dipping the wooden pen's tip in ink.

"Today is the first day of our arrival at Doom and we have been assigned our respective rooms in the central barracks for the chosen ones. We will be assigned our department of work tomorrow and then, officially the second half of the Catharsis will begin till Fatumalism at the end of the Catharsis. But, all our plans of going about with the plan are not going to work now, since I have learned about a potential attack on Mt. Pyrus. It is going to be a chaos, the revelation to the boy has to be made sooner than I had expected. Ever since I left the Pixie

and disguised myself as a shopkeeper in Solvia, I had waited for this day. The deeds and sins of our forefathers have let us go about this journey. I hope to

join the same department of work as the boy and after revealing to him, my duty as a Pixie combatant will be over. May Pixie Forest and our forefathers live long!"

He closed his diary and kept it away. He continued looking out of the window as he had realised by then that he would not be able to sleep that night.

***

Next day, in the province of Tweedle, the training chief was in his shelter alongside the training area when he saw a rider from tenor bureau approaching him. He got out of his hut and walked towards the rider. The horse had a massive yellow symbol indicating the sign of Tenor bureau. The rider dismounted and walked over to the training chief.

"Chieftain Gorm has officially asked you to present him with a small troop of soldiers for the attack." said the rider.

The training chief nodded.

"The troop will be presented by the evening for Chieftain Gorm and I am honoured for the same." said the training chief as he saluted the Rider.

The Rider nodded before mounting his horse and riding away in the direction he had come. The training chief kept standing there with pride and saw the rider riding off his vision. Standing there he looked at the training ground just across the way. He turned around and walked towards the ground. He had never been so proud in years, turning to look at the sun he sensed that it was the time for the final training of the trainees before they were to be sent to Chieftain Gorm. He entered the area, clenched up the sand in his fists, and then rubbed it across his face with a smile.

Ebbe was in the vicinity of his hut trying to collect some woods. He had been trying to collect wood for his mother to cook dinner. His father was looking after the cattle that they had just across their hut. Ebbe sensed someone's footsteps coming from the main huts area

of Tweedle. He stood up to look for the person, his friend and fellow trainee emerged from the bushes. He had been panting and after having some breath, uttered, "Chief...huff, training chief...huff... has called for a final training session."

Ebbe dropped the axe.

"He has called your name. Get ready, Ebbe..."

Ebbe smiled with disbelief and looked at his friend as he retreated back. Ebbe drew a long breath and looked at his parents from a distance. He rushed back to his hut and got inside. Ebbe began to change his clothes as his happiness overwhelmed him. Then he was paused by an unexpected thought. He glanced out of the window, seeing his parents outside. He wiped a tear from his right eye and tried to gather himself. Ebbe walked outside to where his mother was seated, who stood up and was out of breath with overwhelming joy and happiness as Ebbe was there in front of her standing and wearing the final trainees' clothes given to him by the Training Chief bearing the sign of flag of Dumberry on it. He went straight up ahead and hugged his mother. By that time his father had also come there and saw them. They both had never been so proud of their son as they were that day. He uttered," I will take you both out of this, to somewhere where everyone else live among others, like normal people. Enough of you both living like rocks when all you deserve is to be treated like diamonds."

Off he went then from his hut and parents to the training area while his parents watched him, holding each other.

VII

The Shadow of War

Arlan and Bendt had formed a union of fighters to train in Solvia. It had been done so to protect their home from any kind of danger. The families of the chosen ones used to be

busy writing letters to them, while the shop owned by Ramsey remained closed. Arlan was standing at the edge of the Meril, lost in his thoughts while looking deeply towards Pixie Forest. Like his brother, the idea of venturing into the unknown had begun to pique his attention. A voice abruptly interrupted his train of thought as he was about to take a rope and somehow hurl it to the opposite end of the forest. When he looked back, Bendt was approaching him brandishing a stick.

"Arlan, it's time for the training. You are late." He said, throwing a stick to him. Arlan grabbed the stick, waved it around a couple of times, then stomped it on the ground.

"Fine, then."

The others were waiting for Arlan at the other side of the edge. Everyone had a stick in their hand, as Arlan and Bendt approached the training ground.

"We will be learning how to fight with sticks. It's basic, I know. But it's a start", said Arlan.

Pointing to the Pixie Forest, one of the trainees shot back, saying, "Well, I think that the biggest threat we have is from there."

Arlan looked at the direction of Pixie Forest and the looming thought resumed in his mind. Then quickly, he looked away and moved forward by holding the stick tighter.

"Once we have trained enough, no matter what may be there, we can face it."

The others gave a nod and made a circle with their sticks. Arlan turned to face Bendt as he raised his stick in a challenge for a duel. Bendt gripped his stick tightly, then whacked it in the direction of his legs. After quickly parrying the assault, Arlan switched to a defensive stance, managed to maintain his balance, and struck Bendt back. Bendt oversaw the attack and defended himself in time by putting his stick in front of him, thus blocking the attack. Others cheered at looking at them fighting gracefully, while the two continued to fight with their sticks. None of them was eager to kneel down before the other. And so, the spar continued.

They stopped for a break and settled down nearby by sitting on a wooden plank. From the far end of the market, one of Arlan's friends came running towards him to the training area.

"Your mother has called you, Arlan," yelled the friend. Arlan stood up from the plank and gave Bendt his stick.

"Stay frosty. We're not done."
***

The chosen ones were preparing for their commission into different departments of the Doom Kingdom. Ramsey had been awake the whole night with the thought of doing what he was supposed to do. The guards inside the barracks walked around the rooms of the chosen ones to oversee them getting ready. In the meantime, Chieftain Soren had reached outside the barracks with his convoy. The Servicemen opened the gates of the ground of the barracks outside to let the convoy in. Chieftain Soren came down of his horse and after taking a few steps exclaimed," Let it start now!"

All the Servicemen standing on the outside ground saluted him and then together turned to face the barracks. Inside the barracks the chosen ones had been ready with their preparations by then. Then, as the gates were opened, the Servicemen within the barracks whistled. The chosen ones began to come out of their dorms and onto the outdoor ground. Ramsey quickly joined Eve after getting out of his dorm. The two then joined the other who had formed a queue to reach out. All the chosen ones had now reached outside the barracks where chieftain Soren was waiting for them. Chieftain Soren took a few steps ahead as he started to march towards the chosen ones. "You all are here to be deployed into the various departments of the Doom kingdom, to prove your worth and to meet the FULCRUM OF THE DOOM at the end of Catharsis. You, out of everyone could make it till

here because of your hard work and determination. Now remember, whichever department you go into, just do not betray this kingdom, do not betray the FULCRUM OF THE DOOM." said Chieftain Soren as he commanded the chosen ones. Then one Serviceman came marching towards the Chieftain and stood in front of the chosen ones. He then took out a long pamphlet out of his back and opened it.

"There are four departments that one can join to serve in the kingdom of Doom. Tenor bureau, Military, Finance department and department of

Internal affairs. One who wishes to join a department shall come and stand in the different queues pertinent for each department. The first queue shall be for the department of Tenor bureau, second for Military, third for Finance department and the fourth for internal affairs." Said the Serviceman. Chieftain Soren exclaimed, "Let it begin!" as he walked ahead of the Serviceman, who had now moved back. The chosen ones then started to quickly stand up in the desired queues. Eve Looked at Ramsey who looked back at him. They both nodded and then quickly walked towards the queue for the Military. Oliver had joined the queue for Tenor bureau by then. Eve walked up and stood firmly in military queue and behind him stood Ramsey. All the chosen ones had chosen their departments by standing in the queue of the respective department. All the chosen ones were facing chieftain, who after looking at them nodded and then turned to face the Servicemen.

"Members of each department will now proceed to different areas of barrack, from where training will begin soon," said a Serviceman.

***

It was quiet and cold in the area where Centaurs lived in Pixie Forest. Velda had been terrified after discovering the horrifying truth from Murdoch. Murdoch was outside with other male

centaurs doing their routine round ups of the nearby woods. He knew that he had to leave to meet Isidore soon before it was too late. Ludwig had asked him earlier to inform him as well so that he could accompany him as well. During the round ups, Murdoch was aware that he should not let others know about the fact of the attack. When they were about to complete the last leg of their round ups, a thought crossed his mind. He hurried up with others to complete the round-ups. After finishing the round-ups other Centaurs started walking towards their huts while Murdoch stayed back. He took the turn and started walking towards the main huts area where Ludwig lived. Ludwig was with the children near the trees.

"I have been wanting to meet you Ludwig, I need you to do something for me." said Murdoch.

" What is it?" asked Ludwig worriedly.

"I shall go to meet Isidore alone Ludwig, I need you to stay back and look after the Centaurs." said Murdoch.

Ludwig stopped in his tracks.

"I shall join you as well Murdoch, we both need to be there."

" I am worried for my people and I trust you Ludwig. I will return soon, just be with my people."

Ludwig's stoic expression softened into a reassuring nod as Murdoch, the lines of worry etched across his face, released a pent-up sigh of relief. The weight of the moment seemed to lift from Murdoch's shoulders, and gratitude filled his eyes as he realized that Ludwig had understood the gravity of the situation. It was a silent acknowledgment between the two, a bond forged through shared challenges and a mutual understanding of the perils they faced.

(Editor's note: Wow, this is good) With the air coloured with an unspoken energy and the leaves whispering secrets, the forest trail beneath his boots appeared to respond to his mission. The towering trees enveloped Ludwig like old sentinels as he made his way deeper into the woodland, their twisted branches casting ephemeral shadows across his path. Murdoch, in the meantime, spun around with renewed resolve, driven by a sense of urgency and hope. He accelerated his pace and moved in the opposite direction, towards the far-off silhouette of Mount Pyrus. The mist-covered mountain, capped in an ethereal glow, rose up in the distance, beckoning him to a place that was only known to him. Murdoch's objective seemed to be imprinted in every step he took, and every step he took seemed to have a reason. When Ludwig arrived at the Centaur's village, his sharp eyes scanned the terrain. The ancient trees created a captivating scene as the dappled sunlight filtered through them, creating a mysterious aura that permeated the air. Before him, the splendour of the Centaurs opened like a living tapestry. Ludwig took a seat on the mossy ground beneath the branches of a large tree. He found peace in the embrace of nature, with the sound of rustling leaves and whispering winds creating a reassuring melody. Ludwig eased himself, and recollections of his early years suddenly broke through the walls of time. His past was accessible through the enchanted atmosphere of the Pixie Forest. He was surrounded by the warmth of family, the sound of laughing, and the vivid pictures of a simpler time. Ludwig's mind drifted back to the moments he longed to hold onto, the unfettered delights of childhood, the reassuring presence of parents, and the laughter of siblings, all in the quiet peace. The clear memories both as a comfort and a sombre reminder of what he had lost.

Ludwig lived in a tiny provincial town where peace prevailed. His parents had a small piece of land that supported their small hut. They were hardworking farmers with grizzled hands and tender hearts. Their house was surrounded by a patchwork of vivid green fields, with rows of crops that waved gently in the light air like waves of emerald. Ludwig's parents planted the seeds of a future for their family and the neighbourhood they called home. The aroma of rich soil and the prospect of a bountiful crop filled the air, evoking a sanctuary where the natural cycles governed life's rhythm. Their small-town life was infused with a hint of magic by Ludwig's older sister, a passionate painter. She would go into the forest, the old trees bearing testimony to many generations serving as her canvas. She transformed the ordinary into a work of marvel with each brushstroke, creating a silent symphony of colours that danced on the bark. Ludwig would play games with the other kids in the neighbourhood that made everyone laugh aloud. The fields turned into their play area, and in their minds, the borders of the little patch of land could go on forever. Alas...it was not meant to be. Werecats longed for human blood and after secretly quenching their thirst in the Pixie Forest, they ventured into the lands nearby the forest. The first village they got hold of was Ludwig's village.

It was a gloomy night; the moon was full over the village. Some children were playing outside the huts while the elders took care of the annual harvest that they had yielded. However, the peace was broken up north, when the edge of the forest met the village's periphery. From the shadows came two sharp, shining eyes, their light piercing the darkness like ghostly lights. Suddenly, in the shadows of the bushes, a number of eyes blazed like a wicked wave. With an intensity that sent shivers down the spines of those who risked to view the terrible spectacle, they became fixated on the settlement and its inhabitants. Then, from the centre of the charred leaves, one single set of eyes rose, floating above the earth with a strange elegance. The figure that emerged was not your typical beast; it was a Werecat, the forest's sentinel. The Werecat stretched its claws in the dark silence, a menacing glimmer reflected in the moonlight. It swung its paws quickly and gave off a low, terrifying snarl that echoed through the atmosphere. The werecats that had been hiding in the shadows , now sprang out like bloodthirsty beasts.

Their eyes gleamed with an unnatural brilliance that mirrored the malevolence in their intent, as they leapt and prowled, turning the night sky into a canvas for their frightening presence. They were everywhere, their menacing outlines carved against the moonlit sky, behind the overhanging shadows of the trees and on rooftops and in alleys. The Werecats took control, their wild eyes locked on the gullible people, and the air crackled with an electric tension. The peaceful night had become a battlefield of primordial forces in the space of a single glance. The once quiet town was now under the threat of the menacing gaze of the Werecats, who were masters of the unseen, having made themselves known. With its icy, unwavering glare, the moon was a silent witness to the drama that was taking place and would ultimately determine the fate of the town. The battle between innocence and malevolence had begun. The Werecats menacing presence surrounded the villagers and children, causing them to look terrified and let out screams that resounded throughout the night. Infants cried out, and the crowd fell into despair as hopeless attempts to flee exposed the unavoidable reality: the Werecats were everywhere. Heart thumping, little Ludwig dashed through the mayhem, running for his hut. His sister and parents were inside when a prowling Werecat found them, oblivious of the impending peril. It twisted its head, growling menacingly, and charged. Swiftly reacting, Ludwig pounced on the impending danger, resolved to deflect its focus, and protect his family. "Ludwigggg!!!", screamed his mother. Ludwig had reached the Werecat and tried to punch the beat with his hands, but the beast got hold of his hands and threw him off. Upon seeing this, his father came running outside and held the Werecat's legs begging for his child's life. Ludwig was hurt but he quickly got up bleeding from his knees and elbows. By this time, his entire family had come out in front of the Werecat, they were crying and begging for their life. Ludwig quickly ran and stood in front of them to face the beast. The beast twisted his face and smiled and then with a thunderous force stretched his claws out and towards the family. Ludwig's father upon realising their fate held Ludwig in his arms and with all his strength threw him up in the air away from them. In the next moment, the claws of the beast had pierced through their chests. Ludwig landed on the bushes spread across near the periphery of the Pixie Forest, and was blanked out.

Ludwig got up to see the bleak aftermath as soon as his eyes opened. The once-vibrant society was silence by death, and the village lay in ruins, its houses broken. And then, his eyes fell over it. The image of his family, motionless but still clinging to one another. He let out a cry of anguish, tears rolling down his cheeks. He heard a horse charging out of the Pixie Forest in the middle of his sadness. He turned and saw a young Murdoch, a strong Centaur, standing resolutely. Ludwig's shouts had alerted Murdoch, who had come to the scene like a quiet guardian against an unimaginable calamity. Ludwig crying profusely, trusted him immediately and hugged him. Murdoch hugged him back and carried him on his back to take him to Pixie. Since then, he had been a Pixian and later a Pixie combatant. Ludwig woke up from his brief sleep with tears lingering in the corners of his eyes. As he got up, he looked around the area to find the Centaurs safe and sound, a sigh of relief was taken by him.

By then, Murdoch had arrived at the edge of Pixie Forest, where Mt. Pyrus began. He stood there resolutely, gazing up at Mount Pyrus with a twinkle in his eyes. Then he folded his hands, closed his eyes, and began writing on a leaf. He tossed it to the edge of the mountain with great strength in his arm. The leaf fell to the fringes of the shrubbery near the foot of the mountain. A flock of luminescent birds emerged from the base of the mountain up to where Murdoch was standing. Then, with a roar in the sky came flying down, Isidore.

He landed on the edge of the Pixie Forest alongside Murdoch. 'It is good to see you again. Murdoch, isn't it?" asked Isidore.

"It is good to see you again too Isidore." replied Murdoch.

"Dark times are hovering over Mt. Pyrus, Isidore. We have learned that Fulcrum of the Doom is planning an attack on the mountain. Minotaurs and Werecats have also joined their forces."

After hearing Murdoch speak, Isidore let out a squeak and twisted his head, letting off some feathers, "Dark times indeed. The lives on Mt. Pyrus must be saved. May the four lords bestow their blessings upon us."

"Soon, we will be marching our army towards the mountain to surround it. We will take the first blow", said Murdoch.

"We shall fight our enemies together and protect our people", said Isidore. Then, with a puff, he lifted his wings and soared off, returning to Mount Pyrus.

***

Each of the chosen one who had picked their department was brought to a separate dormitory based on that department. Servicemen were giving the briefings regarding the work to be carried out to the chosen ones. Following the briefing, the selected individuals were led to an overhead compartment that housed their training space. Eve walked up to the compartment with Ramsey and the others trailing behind. The Servicemen approached the compartment and then after turning announced," Your training shall commence today itself!!"

Eve felt a surge of adrenaline shoot through his body as he stood there with others as the announcement was being made. One of the Servicemen unlocked the training area's gate. The Servicemen guided the chosen ones to the center as they entered the area. The final

trainees from the province of Tweedle passed through the gate suddenly, which was at the right corner of the area as the chosen ones stood in a straight line. Ebbe was one of them, as he walked up to the position where the chosen ones were standing. Eve caught his sight. He remembered him from the day he had arrived at Doom. Ebbe too recognized him instantly as he walked up towards the position of the chosen ones. The final trainees stood and positioned in front of the chosen ones; both the fractions faced each other. One Servicemen entered the commotion and stood in between both the parties. He took a glance at the chosen ones and announces," You all will be training with these final trainees and they will teach you and make you ready for the military."

VIII

Warriors of Tomorrow

The chosen ones and the final trainees of Tweedle province face each other in the training compartment. Ebbe was one of a total of four final trainees. The Servicemen cleared the area, and the final trainees started to move forward to speak with the chosen ones. It was Ebbe who stepped forward first, drawing a warrior's dagger. With his eyes angled the same way, he said, "Let us train together, fight together, and serve the kingdom of Doom."

With zeal and enthusiasm, the chosen ones held their heads high and exclaimed the same, filling the air with their energy. Ebbe led the squad of the final trainees as each one of them went to the edge of the space to grab a few other accessories. There were two guards stationed outside the compartment, one of them turned around to see what the trainees have been up to this whole time. One of them pointed the other towards Ebbe, as he was

standing in front of the chosen ones. The other guard leaned in slightly to hear what the other had to say.

"I've heard that a Malison is in charge of the last group of trainees."

When the other guard heard this, his eyes opened, and they both turned to look at Ebbe. Ebbe collected every accessory he had previously selected and gave each one to the chosen ones one by one. Ramsey received a bow and arrow; Eve was given a dagger. After every chosen one had received every weapon accessory, Ebbe returned to his original position. Eve tightened his grip on the dagger and peered ahead at the final trainees.

Then, the final trainees walked ahead and stood separately. All four of them commanded together, "Let's make four groups and each of us will start to train a group." The chosen ones started to arrange themselves in four groups. Ebbe looked over the first group and was about to teach them how to combat with a dagger, the second group was about bow and arrow, the third group was about a spear and the fourth group was about a shotel (a curved sword small in size effective for close and hand-to-hand combat). Ebbe took a step backward and began to move his dagger in a wave-like motion across the air. Then he began moving his body in tandem with the dagger, tossing it quickly into the air, turning around from his left side in 360 degrees, and catching the blade with his focused gaze. He then pierced the dagger in the air

"This is known as the Iron Fangs, the deadliest dagger technique. I learnt this from my trainer, and it will undoubtedly kill the opponent."

The guards at the compartment gate kept an eye on the chosen ones as they started their training under the direction of the last trainees. Eve and the others in the dagger group began to replicate Ebbe's movement, just like his body gestures and movements. Eve was doing his best to match with Ebbe's movements as he manoeuvred his dagger as quickly and precisely as he could in the air. The final trainee overlooking the bow and arrow group was teaching them how to hold a bow

and what should be done in regards to putting an arrow precisely to a bow and how to aim it. The chosen ones in the bow and arrow group gestured the motions instructed by their trainer. Ramsey quickly grasped the way to grip the arrow, extended it across the bow, and took aim on his first attempt. He caught the trainer's attention who then swiftly moved toward him and stood behind him. Then with a careful gaze, the trainer inspected his stance of stretching the arrow.

"Impressive. Have you ever done that before?" the trainer asked.

The question lingered in front of him but he wanted to not tell them the reason behind his precision with bow and arrow. He lifted his face and looked at the trainer.

"I had heard about the great warriors wielded with the skill of using a bow and arrow, since then I started to research about this skill." answered Ramsey.

The trainer put his hand on Ramsey's shoulder and said, "For a man of your age, it is rather remarkable." Both of them exchanged smiles and went back to their original positions. The area where both groups were training became charged with energy. There was energy in the air as metal clanged with metal. The trainees of the shotel group moved with the grace of a breeze, trailing their instructor as they launched their assault. Before leaping into the air and launching an assault attack with his spear, the spear group instructor executed a number of rotations. In the meantime, Ebbe was overlooking at how the trainees were holding the dagger and adjusting their grip, if needed. Eve held the knife in both hands before deciding to use his right arm. By gripping the dagger even more firmly, he improved his grasp over the grip, making it ideal for an assault attack. After observing everyone's grip, Ebbe returned to his position. Eve was looking at him eagerly as he had been mighty impressed by the demonstration of the Iron fangs attack by Ebbe. But he had

to wait. From the front gate of the compartment, the Servicemen who had gone earlier returned back. They straight came to the final trainees and stood beside them. Then looking at the chosen ones one of them announced, "This was the introductory training session for all of you where the final trainees got acquainted with you all. Every day, you all will train here under the supervision. You all shall proceed now to your separate dorms for the trainees of the military department."

Upon hearing this the chosen ones started to disperse and walk in a queue of four. The final trainees walked up in front of their respective group and started by leading them. Eve quickly managed to get to initial position of the dagger group and started walking just behind Ebbe. He tried to match the pace with Ebbe who was walking with quite a speed. While, walking up his speed, he tried to get close to him from behind.

"That move that had shown to us, Iron fangs, it was unlike anything I have ever seen", he muttered into Ebbe's ears. Ebbe turned around and looked at Eve.

"Oh, it's you. I do not know if you remember or not, but I had seen you earlier, the day you all were entering the kingdom through the province of Tweedle."

"I remember, you were there by the woods, were you trying to hide something...or someo...", Eve chose not to complete his thought.

Ebbe chuckled a little and continued walking. "It was some private business I had to handle. But yes, you do recall that day quite well. Well, would you have told others about me if you had the chance?" he quickly posed a question back to Eve. Eve, who was interested in having a conversation with him quickly responded with a NO.

"I would not. Maybe I could picture myself in your place that day."

"Now about the iron fangs, the deadliest blow by a dagger ever, is not that easy to learn. it requires precision in every move of it, the grip, the rotation, the speed, throwing it up in the air and catching it in a rhythm. everything requires to be perfect, and remember, it must be

within the fraction of seconds, you ought not to give the time to your opponent. He might end up killing you in the meantime of the rotation. the only way to tackle that is with your speed", said Ebbe. Eve appeared as though he had something from a folklore. The look of astonishment lingered on his face.

They all went through the exit and departed from the compartment. A guard from the pair stationed outside approached and took position in front of them.

"I will now take you all to your dorms of the trainees of the military department." The guard said. The guard ushered them down the lengthy corridor, its walls adorned with portraits of past military trainees. Making a sharp right turn, they stood in front of a sweeping staircase that ascended to their dormitories. Climbing those steps, the massive doors of their living quarters swung open graciously. Stepping inside, the room unfolded before them—a space embellished with grand paintings depicting intricate architecture and imposing statues. The guard then turned and turned to face them; his eyes unwavering. "Welcome to the common dormitory for all military trainees," he said. "The final trainees will stay here. Over there, in separate dormitories, the others will find lodging." He pointed to a hallway that runs along the edge of the common dormitory area. The last of the trainees glanced out over the common dormitory, which would shortly become their common haven. Amid the buzz of activity, they carefully arranged their stuff, making every bunk and locker a blank canvas waiting to be customized. It was a silent moment of expectation, a little break before the hard training that was to come. At the same time, the guard led the other trainees down the hallway that led to the individual dormitories. Eve stepped neatly through the moving queue and was soon walking right behind Ramsey. He was compelled to express his appreciation as they made their way down the dimly lit hallway. "Today was incredible, Ramsey,"

"I was even more impressed by the way you merited your trainer's commendation. For the rest of us, you've set the bar high. I'm excited to study with someone who is so knowledgeable and committed." Ramsey nodded in agreement, enjoying the sense of unity growing among the trainees.

***

It was a breezy atmosphere in Solvia. The market had quite a chatter about the ones who had gone to Doom. People were talking about the kingdoms which perished and the ones which became mighty and prosperous after Fatumalism. There had been many empires in the past which collapsed and perished, the possibility of this was in the fact that people from the adverse group of a particular empire would have made the request in Factumalism that ended the other empire. In their hut, Davina had been keeping a record of days for which Eve had gone to Doom. One year seemed a lot to her, all she wanted was to see her son again. After marking the days on the wall, she returned to her daily chores. She went to the area of her hut where she used to cook. Amidst all her worries and chores, a thought burst into her mind. Magnus's face, the beard he had, the brooding eyes and strong arms. She could not forget that day, the day Magnus left.

"I shall return one day, the day my purpose will complete, I will return Davina."

It had been so many years. But his words had promised her of the hope that someday he would return. But, there was no letter or communication from him.

Arlan was at the stable area of Solvia where all the Solvians kept their horses. Nallbo had been of low spirit ever since Eve had left. Arlan fed some grass to the brooding horse, as Bendt walked into the scene. He was moving erratically and with a lot of energy. He made his way into the stable and found Arlan, who turned to meet his friend.

Bendt sat down, his eyes blazing crimson. Arlan gave him a quick glance before dropping the grass he had been feeding to Nallbo.

"You did it again, didn't you, Bendt?" "Oh! No... I just tried it."

"Well, you have had quite a few tries by now Bendt. Drop it. Now", replied Arlan.

Arlan stood up, picked a basket full of water, and hurled it on Bendt's face and forced him to stand up. The abrupt splash of water over his face caused Bendt to fall. Bendt scratched his eyes and shook his head, opening them wide to see Arlan standing there. Arlan let go of the bucket, grabbed Bendt by the collar, and lifted him up to a seat.

"Never again. Am I clear? Here, take this now and feed Nallbo." Bendt nodded.

Arlan stood up and made his way from the stable. Just across the street, he noticed that the members of his union were wandering the street. Arlan called one of them by their name and made the group turn and look at him.

"What are you up to?" asked Arlan.

"Nothing, just roaming around." replied one of them.

Another one from the group said," We want to fight for real now Arlan, enough with these trainings now."

At hearing it, Arlan grinned and remarked, "I bet you will run away when we will face a real enemy."

The rest of them burst laughter.

"However, I do have a thought," Arlan stated. He had the attention of the bored masses.

"Well, why do not we cross the canyon over to the other side and explore the forest." A long and deep silence engulfed them.

"You must be joking, right Arlan?" one of them questioned at that point. The others gave a nod.

"I'm not".

"Well, you know Arlan, no one has ever gone there, and how would we ever cross the canyon?" replied one of them. Arlan shook his head in disappointment, looking down.

"Well, that was just a thought, I thought you all might agree with me." An awkward silence followed.

"Well then, are we training today?" one of them began, breaking the silence.

"I was thinking of having a day off, you all could train today", replied Arlan. All of them turned and walked out of the street and soon were out of sight. Bendt emerged from behind Arlan, strolling towards the street.

Bendt inquired, "What was that you all were discussing?"

Arlan patted Bendt's head and whispered, "How to make you rid of that thing. Now, come on."

***

Ceannard had summoned the Pixie combatants. Bram was standing directly beneath Ceannard's hut overlooking the combatants. Gazing out the window, Ceannard stood by its edge. There was a threat looming over the forest he had been living in, the area he called

home. He stood looking blankly, and the void in front of him became larger. Bram climbed up the stairs and knocked the door of the hut. The sudden voice of the knock broke Ceannard's concentration. He turned around and walked up to open the door.

"All of them have been summoned Chief." Bram said.

Ceannard nodded and came outside to see all the combatants standing outside waiting for him.

Ceannard glanced at his fighters while gripping the wooden board of his cabin firmly.

"The day has come for all of us to protect our Mt. Pyrus from the enemies. You all will march toward the boundary of Mt. Pyrus and surround it." The combatants listened to him in full glory, while Ceannard continued to address them. "After surrounding the mountain from the base, we shall take the stance with whatever weapons we have."

There was tension in the air, and yet, the combatants did not flinch.

" So, Pixie combatants, it is time for all of us to protect our sacred Mt. Pyrus. But before that, all the children and women including the Centaurs will be taken away from here to a safe spot by Bram. The men who are not fighters will also accompany them."

The combatants knelt and saluted Ceannard.

"Disperse", commanded Ceannard. The combatants set themselves into motion and started to march away from the main huts area. After getting on his horse, Bram rode in the direction of where Murdoch lived. Ludwig was sitting with his eyes closed as before. Ludwig, still resting, heard the sound of a horse approaching. He observed Bram riding towards Murdoch's cabin. He stood up and began to trail behind him. Murdoch, noticing Bram from a distance, emerged from his hut.

Bram dismounted and ambled in Murdoch's direction.

"It is time Murdoch, Chief has ordered for them to be taken to a safe place, away from here." replied Bram.

Murdoch answered, "Yes, it's time. Let me just talk to my wife once."

Bram nodded. Murdoch turned around and entered his hut. Velda had been standing there looking at the door only.

"It is time, isn't it?" said Velda.

"Yes, it is and I need to go and fulfill my duties Velda." said Murdoch.

He came close and hugged her. He touched Velda's belly and caressed it.

"Take care" uttered Murdoch in Velda's ears. Slowly, he let go of her and turned to exit the hut. Ludwig had arrived there in the meantime and was standing next to Bram.

"We shall now report to the Chief. "Said Murdoch.

"The combatants have started to march towards Mt. Pyrus and you both shall assume your positions as well." responded Bram. Then Murdoch reached out and held Bram's hands.

"I know that you are a great leader and you will protect each one of them." Murdoch replied.

Bram replied, "I will with my life." Both of them exchanged the salutes.

"Ludwig, get on, we need to be quick." said Murdoch facing Ludwig.

Ludwig jumped and got on Murdoch's back. When they reached the main huts area. Ceannard was encircled by some combatants and stood in the centre. All of them looked

tense and were looking at a wooden cage which was severed from the middle. Ludwig quickly got down from Murdoch's back and went near the commotion.

"What is it? " asked Ludwig. l"The Werecat. He escaped." Ceannard turned and replied

IX

A Clash of Fates

The Werecats lived in hiding across the right periphery of Pixie Forest, where the forest land ended. It was an uncharted territory, as when the Werecats were vanquished by the Pixians and thrown out of the forest, they had to find somewhere to live. The quench for human blood made them the foe of the people of Pixie Forest and beyond.

It was during that time, when the Werecats made their way out of the Pixie Forest, the nearby villagers of the Pixie Forest had to leave their villages due to the constant fear of being attacked by the Werecats. The escaped Werecat found its way to the borders of the forest. It crossed through the bushes and the concurrent woods to reach the place. It jumped over the trees, hung over the bushes, then jumped onto the ground. The other Werecats came out of the wooden lumber structure.

"Where have you been, Kai?"

"You were there to inspect the area, but you did not come back when you were told to." "I was caught by them", replied Kai.

The others gasped at this revelation by Kai. A relatively larger Werecat started to ascend towards Kai from behind where all the werecats stood. He strode right across them by coercing them to keep aside as he walked.

"What is it that you saw there, Kai?" asked the large Werecat.

"Pantherus...", Kai seemed to regard the large Werecat with reverence, "they have started to march towards Mt. Pyrus and surround it. Also, Isidore has been informed about our attack."

"Hmm, and you told them about our attack, didn't you?" asked Pantherus.

Kai looked down. "They were about to cut my tail....I had no other option. But as soon as, I got the chance I broke the cage and ran away' Pantherus walked towards him and knelt on one knee.

"What do we need to do now, since you have spoiled everything, Kai" asked Pantherus.

Kai with a trembling voice replied," We shall attack first and not give them enough time to set their men."

An evil smile appeared on Pantherus's face as he patted Kai.

"Huhh huh, yes, that is what we will do Kai, I am glad you answered it right, otherwise I would not have forgiven you this time." Said Pantherus.

Then, he turned and looked at other Werecats who had come out of their bushes and wilderness. "Prepare, you all. We will be leading for an early attack", exclaimed Pantherus. The Werecats growled by taking out their fangs like canine and claws out.

The Black hill was filled with the Minotaurs who were honing their weapons, while Vagallath was eagerly waiting for a message from the kingdom. It was a haunting scene to look at there, the ferocious creatures were getting themselves prepared for the attack. Steel and muscle glistened, as the beasts prepared for desolation. Minotaurs were always on the outlook at the nearby forests and other lands for their prey. The quench for human blood was something that made them similar to Werecats. Vagallath came out of his cave and looked at how others had been keeping up with. Every other minotaur was eager to get started with what they were good at: annihilation. Vagallath then quickly moved towards the Draconis peak which had been silent for a long time. Suddenly, a view drew his attention as he was watching over the Draconis peak. An outline of a beast, quick and nimble. A Werecat.

The Minotaurs who were working nearby also left their weapons and stood alongside Vagallath.

Vagallath stood there, looking down at the feline.

"The Pixie combatants have started to march towards Mt. Pyrus. We might need to do an early attack." said the Werecat.

Vagallath's ears perked up as he heard this, all he was waiting for was a green signal to attack. He then rolled his right arm and clenched his fist, making a signal to another minotaur. It went inside the cave and came out with a hawk clamped in his fist. Vagallath turned around to exclaim, "Send the message that we are prepared for an attack." In no time, the Minotaur took a leaf and wrote the message on that, attached it to the claws of the hawk and then sent it up in the air towards the kingdom of Tweedle.

"Tell Pantherus, once we get their reply, we will start marching towards Mt. Pyrus." The Werecat nodded and with its glowing eyes looked around at the minotaurs who came forward towards Vagallath, then stood behind him. Then with a rhythm all of them started to beat their chest. Their growls along with the sound of the chest beating echoed the entire black hill. Vagallath then raised his right arm up in the air with clenched fist, and swiftly opened it. The Minotaurs stopped with their aggression at this.

"Tell him, we are ready".

The Werecat turned around and leapt over from the base of the hill to the nearby branch and began to sprint towards the area of the Werecats.

***

The training had concluded for that day after an entire day of rigorous training. The final trainees and others made their way back to their respective dorms. Ebbe who was in the common dorms area quickly changed into normal clothes. He went outside and sat by a small pond. The guards at the distance looked at him with an interest as he was doing this.

"You are marrying today? Eh, it is enough, you look good." said the guard.

Ebbe turned back and smiled. Then like the whiff of a wind, he slid over on the railing, jumped off it at the base and got down of the barrack area. He mounted his horse from the stable outside and started to ride to the market place of Doom. The streets of the marketplace were bustling with life, while he rode through the streets. People in the streets would have acknowledged Ebbe with a salute, if he was wearing the uniform of final trainees and that could have been a problem for him. Then, he finally saw the way which led to the borders of the Doom kingdom, and from the other side the province of Tweedle started. He pulled the reigns of his horse and started to ride towards that way. There were patches of bushes and on both the sides of the roadway. On the right side of the roadway, Ebbe then looking at the empty road, rode straight towards Tweedle. He stopped at a distance from Elsa's hut and jumped off his horse. He walked up straight towards hut and knocked it. Elsa's mother opened the door.

"What is it that you want?" asked her mother. "I am here to meet Elsa." replied Ebbe.

"What do you think, you can just come to my hut like that and meet my daughter. Do not forget who you are, a Malison", said her mother. Ebbe smiled and took a step forward and said," All these years of shame and prejudice against us, we were told that we are bad bloods, did not even get a proper hut to live in the main huts area. But, not anymore, not anymore. I am the final trainee of the military department of Doom kingdom. Now I want to meet your daughter."

Elsa who had gone somewhere, returned back to her hut and seeing Ebbe and her mother together sent shivers down her spine. She rushed to her mother.

"Elsa, I have come to tell you that I have become the final trainee of the military department and soon I will be in the military. That day, my parents will not live in the woods anymore. They will have a full-fledged hut in the main huts area, and that day, I will come to ask your hand for marriage."

Elsa's mother raised her eyebrows in speechlessness and Elsa stood there spellbound looking into Ebbe's eyes. He too exchanged a glance with her. Then, he turned and headed towards his horse, seamlessly leaving both Elsa and her mother flabbergasted. Ebbe pulled the neigh of his horse, smiled at Elsa and rode back towards the kingdom.

***

Bram had been travelling to the other side of the Pixie Forest with women, children and minotaurs away from the area leading up to Mt. Pyrus. While the others had almost reached the end of the Pixie Forest, and from the other side the base of Mt. Pyrus started. Ceannard was standing facing Mt. Pyrus while Ludwig, Murdoch and other combatants stood behind him. Murdoch stepped forward and stood alongside Ceannard.

"How is Isidore going to accommodate so many of us to the base of the mountain?" Ceannard remained silent.

Murdoch bent down to pick a leaf, Ceannard stopped him. "Don't. Let us just pray. Pray to him."

Ceannard then dropped his spear and folded his hands. Murdoch followed him, which was followed by Ludwig and the rest of the combatants.

"O, Guardian of the Holy Mt. Pyrus, led us the way. Show up for us and lead us to Mt. Pyrus."

Everything went silent around them, not even the rustling of the leaves could be heard. Only their bated breath. Then suddenly, with the whiff of an air, from the bottom of the canyon, emerged Isidore flapping its wings in full glory. Then, turning, he went flying to the mountain.

"Where's he headed" asked one of the combatants. "How could I possibly know that" replied another.

Then Isidore reappeared from the mountainside, soaring and carrying a big tree bough in his beak. The combatants gazed up in amazement as the mighty guardian descended with great force, tossing the massive branch onto the gap that separated Pixie Forest from the foot of Mount Pyrus.

"You all can cross now and reach the mountain foot", said Isidore from up in the air flapping its wings. The combatants rejoiced and Ceannard smiled looking above at Isidore while Ludwig and Murdoch tightened their leg strips ready to lead the pack. Ceannard, looking ahead made a gesture with his right arm to move forward. Then, they all started to march forward to the mountain base, while Isidore flew over them up in the air.

The fairies started to come out of their nests from the mountain with their sparkling wings flapping across the air. The Pixie combatants moved ahead and, on the bough, crossing the large gap that previously did not let them come near the mountain. The luminescent trees up in the mountain near the waterfall, started making voices.

"Why are the fairies coming out of their nests" asked one of the trees as the pink strip started glowing on its branch. "I do not know, they must have seen something." Replied another tree with glowing strips

The Combatants led by Ceannard crossed the large canyon gap and reached the mountain base. The fairies came down to where the combatants were and started flying just above them while glittering sparkles fell from their wings.

"What in good lord, they are amazing." said one combatant. The combatants giggled as the fairies started to fly around them in a circle. The fairies reciprocated with laughter as well.

Isidore looking over them, turned around and flew to the peak of the mountain. Ceannard stopped at the base point of the mountain. From there, to the right of the mountain were the neighbouring woodlands which was not the part of Pixie Forest. This woodland was the way to the Black Hill where minotaurs resided. To the left of mountain was the burned down forest area, which was once very populated with the villages, but once Werecats started residing there the villagers were either slain or they straightaway fled from their villages. This was the place, where the Werecats resided now. And to the back of the mountain was the muddy, patchy way to the kingdom of Doom. Ceannard took a good look around the place, he realised that all the passable three passages surrounding the mountain were that of the enemies and if they attack, they would be surrounded by them with no way out. Then, with a sudden urge his gaze shifted towards the canyon gap that they had just crossed. The thought that what if they somehow make their enemies narrowed down to the edge of the canyon edge, and they fall to their death? This seemed like the perfect plan he could come with, but then he looked at the large bough that had been placed onto the canyon's gap. Now, the only way would be to cover the bough and make them thin at the edge.

Ludwig interrupted his thought by calling his name.

"Ceannard, shall we tell the fairies to go back to their nests?"

Ceannard nodded. He looked around him to see the fairies, who were flying around the combatants. Ceannard fixed the gaze at them and said, "I know, it is very exciting for you all to have us here. But I need you to understand that it is not going to be safe here anymore and you all need to get back to your nests up in the mountain."

The Fairies upon hearing this ceased fluttering their wings and stopped in the air for the moment. Then they looked at each other.

"Yes, you all should return to your nests immediately and do not come out unless we tell you all to."

The fairies looked around and then flew to their nests fluttering their wings up to the mountain. Ceannard held his spear tight and climbed up a boulder placed right in front of him.

"Now, we need to be positioned. Three files will be formed by us; the first file of combatants will be here right at the base of mountain. The second will be ahead and in between of the first layer and the final layer. The third layer will be leading the attack. None of them should get near to the mountain in any case!" exclaimed Ceannard. He walked up to Ludwig and Murdoch. "I will be there in the first layer, both of you shall be in the final layer and do not come ahead in the arena unless I tell you so." Ceannardeagerly looked at them for a yes Both of them nodded and started forming and settling into the layers. Ludwig and Murdoch exchanged glances, and nodded. Ceannard rotated his spear across the air as he moved forward in the final layer. The combatants started to form the layers at the mountain base.

***

Chieftain Soren was in the ministry council at the castle of Doom, briefing everyone about the annual Fatumalism, which was about to begin for that year. A Serviceman rushed through the gate to the inside to meet him. He straight went to him and whispered in his ears, "The minotaurs have sent a message. Pixie combatants have marched towards the mountain."

Soren turned his head. He made a sign to the Servicemen to go away. "That was rather unexpected"

"The annual Fatumalism is going to take place soon", said the Serviceman.

"King Ulrik should be there for the back-up. Send the final trainees and they can choose two of the military trainees to go with them," said Soren.

"But, they have just arrived, their training has not even completed."

Soren turned his head quickly and looked at him and said, "It is a good opportunity to...cut the weak. Elimination should be done from now on, it is a good opportunity. Dol what has been said and send them to join forces with minotaurs and werecats with immediate effect."

Soren held his head up and started walking towards the Fulcrum's mansion in the castle to meet Lord Odan. The Serviceman saluted him and then turned to rush to the common dorm area for the trainees of the military department. All the trainees were getting ready for their training at the training compartment. The Serviceman rushed through the long corridors to the common dorms area. Ebbe along with other final trainees were alerted by the unexpected visit of a Serviceman, who directly stood right in the middle of the common dorms area. All of the final trainees stood up and looked at him to know the reason of his visit. Meanwhile the other trainees also assembled there.

"Consider yourself extremely lucky. You have been granted the chance to serve the king of Doom and Fulcrum of the Doom with your blood and sweat today. You all are assigned the task to go to Mt. Pyrus and join forces with the clans of minotaurs and werecats in their fight against the traitors living on the mountain. And, trust us, those who perform extremely well, will be directly promoted and his chances of appearing in the next fatumalism will increase tenfold. You all can take any two of the trainees under you with you to assist, and we know that their training has not been finished yet, but it is a fact of honour that you all are getting a chance to prove yourselves, and remember those who come back with success

will be directly sent for the next fatumalism. Your war uniforms are there just outside of the dorms area. You do not have much time. Go and serve the Fulcrum!"

All the trainees saluted him as he left the dorms area. Ebbe turned towards Eve. "You will be going with me", then turned to another trainee of the dagger group and said, "You too."

Ramsey had shivers in his spine as the news that Mt. Pyrus is going to be attacked was just announced in front of him. The final trainee of the bow and arrow group called his name and another trainee's name to accompany him. As Ramsey turned pale, Eve came and stood near him. He looked joyous and had been smiling since his name had been called by Ebbe.

"I couldn't even imagine that we would get to work for the kingdom so soon, what do you say Ramsey?" asked Eve. Ramsey looked at him with a dead face and muttered, "We need to go there, very soon, very soon , Eve."

Eve smiled and said, "Yes, Ramsey, I am glad we are in this together."

All the other final trainees had also selected the those who would accompany them. They all rushed out of the dorms area to find their uniforms. The war uniforms were there ona long wooden table. There were hoods, kerchiefs and long dapper like uniform with a hood on its top. The brown leather belts went across the uniform firmly holding it. Daggers, shotels, spear and bow and arrow were also present right beside every uniform. Eve began donning the uniform. It had been a long time since he had a haircut, so he took a thread out of his pocket and started to bind his hair. Others too were quick with donning the uniforms.

Ebbe checked all the daggers which were there and picked three of them.

"Hey, Eve", Ebbe exclaimed from a distance and threw the dagger at him. A startled Eve caught it by holding it right in front of his face.

Ebbe smiled.

"That's for you".

All the trainees had worn their uniforms. They all rushed to the stable outside and got on their horses. Ebbe was in the middle of the entire riding commotion. "For the kingdom of Doom" shouted Ebbe, as all of them pulled the neigh of their horses and started their ride towards Mt. Pyrus.

X

The Clash at Mt. Pyrus

The Pixie combatants had formed the tri-layer to protect Mt. Pyrus. Ceannard was there in the first layer leading them. The fairies had settled back in their nests, and the entire mountain had gone silent. All the combatants had their spears ready on the ground in front of them. Ludwig looked around the entire area in anticipation of anything suspicious, but there was nothing. Murdoch left the last layer and walked up towards Ceannard and leaned towards his ears.

"I do not think that they would take this much time. They might be around here somewhere in hiding." Ceannard considered the possibility.

Eve along with others were riding with all their might towards Mt. Pyrus, they had already covered a considerable distance as now the mountain peak was visible. The sound of the hoofbeats created by the running of the horses echoed in the air as they neared towards the mountain. They had already bypassed the way to Dumberry by taking the straightway route to the mountain. Now, the periphery of the mountain could be seen. As they drew closer, Ramsey grew paler. There was a narrow passage the area they were travelling to the mountain. They entered the passage one by one and continued to move forward to reach the foot of the mountain.

Suddenly, they stopped. The ground began to tremble. Ebbe dismounted, and quickly put his ear on the ground. The trembling seemed to be increasing. He got up and hopped onto his horse.

"We do not have much time; it seems that the minotaurs and werecats are getting closer to the mountain base. We need to hurry". Said Ebbe while pulling his horse's neigh and going ahead. The rest of them followed him in close pursuit.

The Pixie combatants were startled with the shaking of the ground, Ceannard looked around to find where the enemies might be coming from. Suddenly, distinct shouts could be heard from both the sides of the mountain. All the combatants turned to look in the direction of the voices. The fairies sneaked out of their nests to look down as to where the voices were coming from. Then, a loud growl from the right side of the mountain pierced the entire surrounding. All the combatants turned right to look and saw Vagallath standing there with his army of minotaurs. The evil smile on his face intensified as he turned the greataxe in his hand. Ludwig and Murdoch stood firmly, preparing for Ceannard's signal to attack. Then, all of a sudden, very high-pitched purrs screeched through the air. The combatants turned around and found Pantherus standing there with the Werecats.

"We have been surrounded from both the sides" thought Ceannard, as he started to sweat. They were just getting prepared to face the enemies from both the sides, Ebbe and others emerged from the narrow passage through the woods. Now the combatants stood surrounded by the enemies from all the three sides. Eve curiously came forward and stood beside Ebbe. He started to look around and the magnificent Mt. Pyrus caught his attention. Vagallath looked at Ebbe, who looked back.

"We are from Doom." shouted Ebbe. Vagallath upon hearing this smiled and then looked straight at Ceannard and his army. The sheer horror of being surrounded by the enemies engulfed the combatants, Murdoch put raised his arm said, "Do not let your guard down, combatants, we are here to protect Mt. Pyrus. And we will".

Vagallath snarled and shouted, "Then die protecting it!" He growled as the monstrous beasts began to charge. Pantherus unleashed his claws and signalled the werecats to attack. Both these armies sprinted towards the combatants who were in the middle from both the sides.

"It is the time. Let's go!", said Ebbe' looking at other trainees. All the military trainees held their weapons tight and rushed to the battleground. Eve emerged in the front from behind and started to rush towards the arena. Ramsey too joined Eve in sprinting ahead from the rest of the group. Ceannard screamed and with his spear, started giving deadly blows to the minotaurs, piercing their hard-shell body. Werecats started to jump to a considerable height as, they successfully breached the first layer. Kai with other werecats landed just in front of the combatants of the second layer. Kai aimed for the necks of the combatants and killed a couple of them instantly. Ebbe slid across the ground and entered the middle of the battleground. Eve too hurried behind him, taking out his dagger, he started to aim for an attack. Ebbe without wasting any time, took out his dagger and while sliding on the ground with his knees, cut through the legs of a combatant. Soon, blood started to soak into the ground as the battle intensified. The other military trainees had also started to attack the combatants. Ramsey kept running and did not stop to attack like other. Ceannard quickly spotted him and shouted his name, Ramsey turned to look at him and nodded. Then, swiftly picking out an arrow, stretched it across bow and shot it towards the Werecats, by jumping and turning towards them simultaneously. The arrow pierced the heads of three werecats together. The final trainee of the bow and arrow group stopped attacking in shock and yelled, "What are you doing Ramsey?

You are attacking our allies." Ebbe too got up from the ground and looked at Ramsey. Eve who was just preparing to attack, too looked at Ramsey.

"Ramsey, what is it with you?" asked Eve. "You will get to know soon." Replied Ramsey while shooting an arrow.

Ludwig looked at Eve for the first time as he was talking to Ramsey. But Ludwig was not sure whether he was the one, the next Fulcrum of the Doom.

Pantherus was swift with his attacks using claws and piercing through the chests and necks of the combatants leading to their instant death. Murdoch with the desire to go upfront and fight was making him restless, but he and Ludwig were following Ceannard's orders. Eve quickly turned away from Ramsey and gripped his dagger to attack a combatant who was approaching towards him. He rotated his dagger and then when he was just about to attack the combatant, an arrow perforated the combatant's neck. The final trainee of the bow and arrow group had shot. Vagallath had unleashed his inner beast, using his bonish boulder weapon, he started to smash the combatants. The combatants soon turned into a huge puddle of blood by the deadly blows of Vagallath. The first layer was almost destroyed, as most of the combatants were dead. Ceannard was battling away with the Werecats, who with their extraordinary ability to jump had climbed over to his shoulders to attack him. Suddenly, a group of werecats and minotaurs came running towards the mountain holding a large stone. Then, together with all their mighty strength threw it over to the nests of the fairies in the mountain.

"Nooooo" shouted Ceannard, as he took an aim and threw his spear towards the werecats holding the stone, killing them instantly. Some of the fairies startled with the attack, came out of their nests screaming in fear. One of them, a young fairy lost her sense of direction and came flying down to the battleground. Eve who was still struggling to blow an attack,

started looking around him to get an opportunity to pounce on someone. The fairy started flying haphazardly, trying to avoid any attack. Suddenly, Eve appeared in front of her in the battleground. The moment froze, as Eve and the fairy looked at each other, into each other's eyes like a trance. Looking at the fairy, made Eve realise of his childhood when he had seen a fairy for the first time. The moment, at which his awe of going to the Pixie Forest had started. Their moment was suddenly crushed as an arrow came from behind, splitting through the back of the fairy. The fairy fell down to her death. Eve stood there, frozen, looking at the lifeless body of the fairy. The other fairies who were still in the sky started wailing looking down at the body of the dead fairy. Then, all of a sudden, a rage a fire ignited from the inside of Eve. He looked at the trainee who had shot the arrow, a trainee of the bow and arrow group. The dagger he had been holding for so long, seemed very light at that moment. He threw the dagger in the air, then rotated 360 degrees and caught the dagger at the exact tandem of the moment and skewered the trainee's chest (Iron fangs), who then fell on the ground lifeless. The entire military trainees looked at Eve in utter shock and disgust. Ebbe sprinted towards him from the behind and pushed and tossed him on the ground. Ebbe was on top of Eve when he clenched his fist in rage started punching Eve.

"What is it with you two? You traitors." Exclaimed Ebbe while punching Eve. Ludwig quickly got through the fighting commotion and held Ebbe by his waist. Then, with the sheer strength of his arms lifted Ebbe up and tossed him to the other side. Ludwig stretched his arms to Eve, who got up in his feet with the help. Then, a loud noise came from where the first layer had been keeping up with the enemies. Almost all of the first layer was gone, only Ceannard and a couple of combatants were alive and fighting. Murdoch had been keeping up for so long, he could not wait for the orders anymore. A large boulder came flying towards the second layer, crushing a few combatants to death. Vagallath jumped on top of it and started throwing rocks at the heads of the combatants.

Eve did not know why he killed the fellow trainee, but somehow it felt right to him. On the other side of the mountain base, the werecats had started to form linear vertical structure to reach nests of the fairies. Murdoch had closed his eyes for a bit to internalise the screams of the combatants. Then, with a towering rage opened his eyes and he jumped from the position he was standing. He went to the other side to tackle werecats, sprinting with his four legs. He extended his arms wide open and then after getting near the base of the formation of the werecats, held their legs and propelled to other side and dashed them on the ground. The remaining Werecats came down and started surrounding Murdoch, all of the beasts took their claws out and growled at Murdoch. Kai was one of them, he charged towards Murdoch who had his back on Kai. Murdoch's ears perked on hearing the footsteps of Kai running towards him. Kai jumped towards him pointing his claws to his neck, Murdoch's right arm raised, and he turned too to face Kai. Then by raising the first two legs, Murdoch raised and kicked Kai like a thunderbolt . Kai went sliding on the ground like an insect. The other werecats, seeing this feat, ran away. Pantherus was fighting like a cat possessed, his claws piercing through metal and flesh. Ludwig, who had shoved Ebbe away from Eve saw Pantherus, who was approaching towards him. The first glance at him, at his eyes made Ludwig shake with horror. The horrors of his past, the same eyes he had seen, that night, that fateful night when his family and entire village was annihilated by the werecats. He stood there, just looking at Pantherus, who had taken out his claws aiming towards Ludwig. Pantherus took a leap forward on Ludwig, but was intercepted by Eve who punched him at the right time.

"What are you doing, just standing there," said Eve.

Ludwig got back his senses, his breath speared out fire, that fury he had for so long, since his childhood. He grabbed a shotel from the ground and marched towards Pantherus, who was

on the ground. Ludwig pounced on him and attacked him with his shotel, but Pantherus narrowly escaped it by rolling over to the other side. Ludwig did not give up and went after him. Pantherus got up and started to walk around Ludwig, who too was following his trail. Suddenly, the sky above made a loud noise, the colour of the sky started to change to a palette of palette of red. Ceannard who was fighting, exclaimed, "The Fatumalism has started."

And then, a shrill caw. From the mighty red sky, emerged Isidore. Ceannard rejoiced on seeing him while continuing fighting. Isidore came down to the battleground and held some of the minotaurs in its claws, then took a flight to the canyon's gap and threw them down into the chasm. The minotaurs fell on the ground disgruntled and started to go to the other side. Isidore flapped his wings again and took a flight down to the rest of the minotaurs. It appeared in front of them from the sky and instantly severed their heads by drawing out its claws. Next were the Werecats, who had begun forming their vertical linear structure to reach to Isidore, with the hope of taking him down. Eve, finding his place in this grand conflict, started to deliver deadly blows to the werecats and minotaurs. Ludwig had Pantherus choking in his arms, and even as Pantherus dug his claws into Ludwig's arms, the man adamantly held on. Then Pantherus pierced his claws in Ludwig's right thigh., which made Ludwig scream in pain and his grip loosen. Pantherus jumped, and with a hard punch tossed Ludwig to the ground. Pantherus's ears perked as he heard trailing of a horse, all of a sudden from his left, Murdoch emerged, who while still in the air with the momentum generated from his jump, and kicked Pantherus on his chest, Pantherus flew over and landed on the ground after sliding for a considerable distance. Murdoch then helped Ludwig get up.

"You got this, Ludwig."

Both of them turned aside with their backs supporting each other and punched the forthcoming werecats together. Isidore had been taking out the enemies, but he did not see

that behind him, a linear vertical structure was formed by the Werecats. Vagallath came running and hopped on to the structure and started climbing up the structure. He reached the pinnacle and leapt forward towards the back of Isidore. Isidore screeched a bit when Vagallath got hold of the feathers. A high-pitched shrill screech was made again by Isidore as Vagallath started to tear apart his feathers. Ceannard looked up at the wailing Isidore as the minotaurs and werecats started to rejoice.

"Isidoreeee", screamed Murdoch who was middle of an attack. Eve too, who was standing close to where werecats were trying to get hold of the shrubs at the base to climb up. Eve looked distress to look at the lamenting Isidore.

"We have to help him," said Eve.

Right next to where Eve stood, Ramsey took out the arrows and started shooting at Vagallath. Meanwhile, to the other side of the battleground Ludwig and Pantherus were putting up a fight.

"You shall die today, here, then only the death of my family and the villagers will be avenged", said Ludwig looking straight at Pantherus.

"I cannot remember, as so many humans I have killed, human blood that I have quenched cannot be forgotten. I shall kill you too today." Pantherus replied pointing towards Ludwig. Ludwig yelled and charged towards Pantherus with all his force. He jumped and gave him a powerful blow of punch, Pantherus was retrieved back due to the punch, who stood back up and held Ludwig's arms, trying to break them. Ludwig yelled in pain as Eve came running from behind and jumped over the two of them, while in the air he dropped his dagger into the right arm of Ludwig. Then with great force, he manged to get his right arm out of the hold. Swiftly, he moved his arm to the right and started to stab Pantherus repeatedly. Then, he threw the dagger up in the air, held Pantherus with his

left fist, caught the dagger with his right fist and stabbed him right in his throat. Blood streams started pouring out of his throat as he fell on his knees holding the throat.

"This is for my family, my people, my childhood." Eve walked up to a panting Ludwig and saw Pantherus in his last moments.

"That was brutal, he deserved that." Said Eve. "Yes, he really deserved that." Said Ludwig. Eve extended his hands for a handshake and Ludwig proceeded back with a handshake.

"We have known about you, for so long, it is good to see you finally. Don't worry, you will get to know what it is about.", said Ludwig. Suddenly, they heard the screams of Isidore coming from above. Vagallath sat atop a bloodied Isidore. Upon hearing the wailing of Isidore, a few fairies flew out of their nests towards Vagallath. They quickly surrounded him started to hit him in the eyes with pointed sticks they had brought from the nests. Vagallath tried to make them go away, but the fairies were able to escape his attacks. One fairy took the stick and inserted it in his right eye blinding Vagallath in one eye, vagallath screamed and after getting out of balance fell down from Isidore's back on the ground. The minotaur screamed and fell off, right back onto the ground.

Ramsey had been running and climbing up to the shrubs nearby to aim at the enemies, what he did not know was that Kai had been following him from behind all along waiting for the perfect opportunity to attack. Ramsey took out an arrow and stretched it, suddenly Kai took a jump from above, turned around and landed in front of him. In a swift move, his sharp claws ripped through Ramsey's chest. Ramsey fell down to the ground holding his chest.

"Ramsey!" shouted Murdoch. He rushed to him and held him in his arms. Ramsey somehow managed to take out the diary from his back pocket of his uniform and gave it to Mudoch.

"Give this to him, to Evander and tell him how, how... much we need him to win this war against the Lord", murmured Ramsey.

"I will, Ramsey, just hold onto sometime, you will be fine." Said Murdoch.

Ramsey smiled.

"I have fulfilled my duty as a Pixie combatant, Murdoch. I feel cherished. Take my body back to the forest. Please. Promise me."

Ramsey felt silent then, his hands turned pale and hung like a ripened fruit about to fall. Murdoch slowly closed his eyes and took his body to the nearby shrub and put his body under it.

Suddenly, a layer of mist started to float down from the peak of the mountain to the battleground. The mist started to get dense, and soon it engulfed the entire area. Nothing could be seen as the mist was everywhere on the battleground, covering the view. Then, a huge gush of wind came from within the mist and swept away the minotaurs and werecats to the canyon's gap. The beasts got startled by this, then a loud noise of flapping of wings could be heard from within the mist. The mist started to form a circle with rapidly. The minotaurs started to run away from it but, another layer of mist ascended down from the other side to where the minotaurs ran. The blanket of the mist pushed them back to where they had come from and eventually, they were cornered near the canyon's gap. Then a large serpent formed of the mist charged towards them, and pushed the minotaurs to their death. Then large wings emerged from the mist and they seemed to start flapping. Then the covers of mist started disappearing from the ground, Anaira flew above with her wings.

Ludwig gasped. "That is Anaira." Eve looked up in awe as well. Anaira made a round gesture with her hands and then a ball of mist started generating within her hands. It became very large and began to rotate, and as Anaira opened her fist, and released the humongous ball of mist towards the minotaurs, that massive ball of mist engulfed the remaining minotaurs inside it and vaporised them. Vagallath started trembling with fear as he stood just in front of Anaira from a distance. Kai along with other werecats stood behind Vagallath

alongside other minotaurs. Anaira took a step forward, while her huge wings stretched out entirely. Vagallath shrieked and made a huge noise from his throat, an attempt to intimidate Anaira. Anaira started stepping forward while fluttering her wings, as the beasts began to step back. Again, a layer of mist started to emerge from her behind, Vagallath seeing it set his right foot in motion and turned around. He quickly pounced to go to the other side. Ebbe and other military departments tried as well but they were left behind as other minotaurs and werecats joined Vagallath first. Ebbe stepped back from the commotion and turned to look at Eve.

"I will kill you with my own hands, traitor, I cannot believe I trusted and brough you here. Like your other friend, you will be dead too."

Eve looked at him without being able to comprehend whose death Ebbe was talking about. He started to look around startled.

Murdoch looked at him and said, "Ramsey."

Eve felt his heart skip a beat. Rising his head up with red eyes filled with anger, Eve asked, "Who did it?"

Murdoch replied, "The Werecat who escaped from our clutches, called Kai."

Suddenly, a huge roar and growl broke the air. A huge dragon with tremendous wings started ascending down towards the mountain base. A tall, brooding man with subtle beard, medium-sized hair and blue eyes, leaned onto the right side to look down, he seemed to be riding the dragon.

Anaira looked up as well and whispered, "Lord Odan."

XI

An Oath of Vengeance

"Lord Odan" reiterated Ceannard as a sense of fear started to grapple him. The huge dragon flew over them with elasticity as if it were dancing in the air,.

"Retreat" yelled Lord Odan from the back of dragon.

"Retreat, all of you!" Lord Odan yelled again. The onlookers on the ground started to disperse on the instructions by Lord Odan. Vagallath signalled his army by his fist and they started to march swiftly to the forest side, where they had come from. Werecats looked haphazardly confused as Pantherus was dead. Kai stepped forward and looked at them. He too quickly signalled them and started to march out of the battleground. The dragon's wings were expertly angled as it got closer to the ground, changing pitch to regulate its fall. The noise resounded through the hills and valleys below as the wind whipped past the enormous body of the dragon, reaching a crescendo. The dragon was so powerful that the ground trembled as it got closer, demonstrating the strength of its muscular body. Ebbe upon looking at Lord Odan for the first time knelt down in respect, he could not believe his eyes, and looking at Ebbe other military trainees too did the same. Anaira walked up and stood in front of Ceannard and other combatants, while Murdoch and Ludwig went to the opposite sides to stop minotaurs and werecats from leaving.

"You both, "combatants" huh...., come back here now." Said Lord Odan.

Lord Odan mounted down from his dragon. His long black cape that he was wearing fluttered, as he started walking ahead. Anaira stood in front of him from a distance.

"I did not know, that I would have to come by myself. I thought the minotaurs and werecats were capable enough to do the work, you know, the quench for human blood can make them even do the impossible. But this time...they failed." Anaira shrugged.

"I will not let you do what you have come for." She turned around in rotation and flapped her wings, and released a huge ball of mist towards Lord Odan. Lord Odan unflinched just stood there and snapped his finger. The entire mist ball evaporated, then he turned to look for Eve. Eve stood there with fear and curiosity as he could not have ever imagined to see Fulcrum of the Doom so soon in this journey of his, but then the thought that the whole attack on Mt. Pyrus was orchestrated by him made him confused. He did not know why he turned his back on the Doom kingdom, the moment he did that, he could only think of the dead fairy in front of him. Lord Odan looked at the combatants and in front of them stood Eve, Ludwig, Ceannard and Murdoch. Lord Odan tried to recognize Eve among them. He gazed through all of them one by one, but then his eyes saw Eve. Same face he remembered, same eyes, same hair colour. Lord Odan's eyes gleamed as he pointed his finger at him.

"You, you must be the one. Magnus's son." Said Lord Odan.

Eve's eyes got wide opened as dubiety framed his face. A flow of questions started to run inside his mind.

"How do you know that name, Lord Fulcrum?" asked Eve.

Lord Odan smiled and replied, "Just know, it had to be done, for the world, for the generations to come."

"What?" asked Eve eagerly.

"No! It did not!", intervened Anaira who was standing in a distance. Lord Odan turned towards her, twisted his face and said, "I need to hurry back, Fatumalism has to be done." Then, he closed his eyes, raised his arms and then clapped with force. A huge gale moved towards Anaira, who saw it and started producing a ball of mist. Ceannard on seeing this pounced and sprinted towards Anaira, but a gale redirected towards him as well. The gale transformed into a huge dragon like persona. It attacked ceannard and he was taken to the other direction by the persona. The mist ball, Anaira created throttled and clashed with the force of wind but was overpowered. The force of wind did not stop, Anaira started shooting mist balls towards the wind force but in vain. Then, suddenly Eve came running and stood in front of Anaira with stretched arms. Lord Odan murmured, "Just like his father." The gale hit Eve who was tossed around by the dominant force. Ceannard and others ran towards Eve, as Anaira fluttered her wings and went straight to Lord Odan flying. Lord Odan held his cape and swiftly whirled it around, a ring of fire got generated and the flames started getting higher and aggressive. Anaira tried to block the fire with her wings, but was overpowered by the heat. Then, a huge layer of black mass started emerging from the back of Lord Odan, it got high and soon with the speed of a thunderbolt surrounded Eve and others. Lord Odan grinned and hopped onto his dragon.

"Nooooo" screamed Anaira, as she saw Lord Odan taking the flight on his dragon towards the mountain peak. As the dragon's red eyes looked straight at the mountain peak, the right wing of the dragon got ripped by an attack by the claws of Isidore. Isidore soared high and turned to the other side to attack Lord Odan as well. Lord Odan dodged the attack by bending down, then the dragon lifted its tail and with a great force hit Isidore. Isidore tried to elude it but could not, his right wing got severed and he yelled in pain.

"Isidore, Isidore" screamed Anaira from the ground.

Isidore struggled to continue flying with one injured wing, but soon he started to lose the balance. The dragon flew over and reached the mountain peak. Lord Odan jumped down onto the ground in front of the massive trees which led to the waterfall. The stirps on the trees started to glow up as Lord Odan headed towards the waterfall. The huge branches of the trees started to grow large, then stretched and moved out to block the way of Lord Odan.

"Do not let him through, stay together, hold on" said one tree. The other trees glowed and the branches on the trees started to stretch out in wicked shapes, soon the branches turned into a web and blocked the entire way. Lord Odan stopped walking and stood ferociously in front of the webbed branches.

'All of you are the long-gone souls. I do not want to imply my force and hurt you all. Clear my way, understand that Fatumalism is the way of life," said Lord Odan.

The Trees did not move a bit and the branched remained unmalleable. Lord Odan took a long deep breath and then started to walk forward towards the trees. A black mass started to emerge from his back and transformed into the shape of two humongous arms, the arms extended and held the branches. Then, as Lord Odan walked ahead the, the arms stretched the branches open. The anguished trees could not hold their strength anymore and gave up eventually. The glowing strips on the bark of the trees turned pale. Lord Odan continued to walk ahead, and in a while, he reached at the waterfall. Lord Odan closed his eyes and, in his mind, started to map the way which led to the place for which he had planned all this: the tomb. The only thing which had been bothering him for so long. He raised his hands and made a gesture to divert the flow of water running in the waterfall. The waterflow got diverted to both the sides and a way forward was made. Lord Odan walked past through it

and crossed the waterfall. There it was, what he had been looking for. The Tomb. He proceeded further towards the tomb, all of a sudden, a veneer of heavy mist hovered above the ground and started ascending down. From the left side of the peak appeared Anaira fluttering her wings. She flew over him directly and tried to attack him. Lord Odan bent down to abstain from the attack, the blow landed straight to his right cheek. Lord Odan got up fuming with anger, raised his arms, circled them and then shot a fireball towards Anaira. Anaira got hit by the fireball and the impact was such that she fell down from the peak. When Eve and the others on the ground noticed Anaira tumbling down from the peak, they were alarmed and tried to arrange themselves to catch her. Lord Odan looked at the tomb and noticed the words scribbled on it. He again mage a gesture from his arms and shot a fireball at the tomb. The upper structure of the tomb got shattered into pieces. The loud sound of the attack explosion sent trembles to the ground below. Anaira got up and looked at the peak, she saw Lord Odan coming down on the ground again.

"I had given the minotaurs and werecats a chance to devour the lives of Mt. Pyrus, but alas, they could not. But the tomb has been destroyed", said Lord Odan from above sitting on his dragon. He looked down at Eve.

"I could kill you right now, but I will not. As the Fulcrum, I have my morales. But I know you will find a way to me one day, and then not as the Fulcrum but as Odan, we shall fight."

Then, his dragon wagged the wings and took a flight up in the sky. At that point, Ebbe and other military trainees were on their horses and started to return back to Doom kingdom. While riding back, Ebbe yelled, "Evander, I will kill you with my own hands." Then after neighing the horses, they all went ahead."

"I failed to keep his promise." uttered Anaira.

With a rage in his eyes, Eve stepped forward and asked, "What is it all about?"

Anaira whirled around and a mist cloud formed. All of them stepped on it and the cloud started hovering upwards to the peak. Soon, they reached at the waterfall, and stepped down. They walked up to the tomb, which had been destroyed from above.

"This is where he was buried, your father. Magnus Leopold."

"He was able to gather the power to write the fate that cannot be changed even by the Fulcrum, due to the blessings of Lord Amandus. He had done the holy pilgrimage to all the four lords, which was done by Lord Odan as well. But your father always believed that fate cannot be controlled, it should not be controlled, the fruits of one's hard work should determine their fate, not Fatumalism. This led to the great war of Gaelic Valley. Pegasuses also helped Magnus in this war, but our defeat determined the course of the world.

The Pegasuses were the ancestors and forefathers of Centaurs. But, when he was dying, Magnus came here and with that one blessing forged the fate of ending Fatumalism, in which you were to end the tyranny and become the next Fulcrum of the Doom. Magnus bounded the seal of the fate with his tomb, but I failed to protect it."

Eve took out the locket, his father had left for him and with tears in his eyes sat down near the tomb.

"Those who supported Magnuses were killed, but those who survived were taken to the kingdom of Doom. They were named as "Malisons", the bad blood. Now, it is your journey, you need to go out and complete the holy pilgrimage, Lord Odan will be watching you at every step, trying to kill you." said Anaira.

"Ramsey, had always been a Pixie combatant. He was sent to Solvia to be with you, look after you if you are selected for the catharsis", said Ceannard with tears in his eyes.

Eve got up, wiped his tears and looked at Ceananrd, Ludwig and Murdoch.

"I will, I will do it. I will put an end to this tyranny and avenge the death of my father, Ramsey and all other combatants. I, Evander Leopold, pledge this unto my death."

"This is all the information I could help you with, you need to travel and meet the heirs of Sophie. Queen Sophie was an important part of the rebellion. The most fierce and skilled warriors, heirs of Sophie are, all of them are women, but the hatred they faced by men, made them flee the land and adopt the ways of sea. They now sail and keep rescuing women on the lands from the clutches of the evil men, putting an end to their suffering."

Eve looking resolute clenched his fist, walked up to the edge of the peak from where they were standing. Then looked ahead, to the huge Doom castle which was far away, but still visible. The dragon flew over to the castle, Eve took a huge, deep breath and said, "The war for Doom has just started."

To be continued.......

IN

THE AGE OF FOREFATHERS: BOOK TWO OF THE DOOM TRILOGY

● 97 ●

The air had started to feel heavy and lousy at the mountain foot as the dead combatants' bodies lied around everywhere and some from the remaining ones were busy counting the deaths, while others dragged the dead bodies to a common spot. It had been around some time, since Eve and others had gone to the peak. One of them started checking around the shrubs to look for any injured combatant who might have been stuck there. The combatant touched upon Ramsey's body in the shrubs while searching, his hands went deeper into the shrubs to get a better hold of the body. He held it tightly and started pulling it outside from the shrub. Others were busy making beds for the corpses to be carried to the Pixie Forest out of the fallen wood stakes on the ground. One of the combatants made a loud whistle while looking at the Pixie Forest. A hawk emerged from the woods and flew down over the combatant and sat on his right arm. A message had been inscribed on a leaf by the combatant on the orders of Ceannard. The hawk looked around with frantic head movements and then clenched the leaf in its claws and took a flight towards the depth of Pixie Forest.

Bram and other Pixians had been residing in the other half of the forest since the battle started. Velda, female centaurs along with other female Pixians had prepared some food for other Pixians, meanwhile Bram and other combatants were keeping a watch at the frontiers of area where the children, women and old were kept, away from the sight of the enemies. The chatter about the battle was becoming louder, as every teenage Pixian was coming up with his own story of the battle scenario and how many enemies would have been killed by then. Velda holding her belly kept looking at the sky, thinking of when Murdoch would return from the battle. Other women centaurs were there as well, praying to Pegasus. The sense of dread had taken over them, but a ray of hope glimmered in their eyes as well. The children of centaurs constantly looked at the sky while making and thinking of ways to get a bit far from the commotion. Suddenly, one of the young centaurs saw a hawk flying down and coming their way. He started shouting while looking and pointing at the hawk, "There's a hawk coming this way, look! a hawk!" shouted the child.

Bram and other combatants turned around and looked above at the hawk descending towards them on the ground. The hawk flew down quickly and landed on the right arm of Bram. Bram untangled the thread and took out the leaf from its claws, unrolled the leaf and read,*"The war's over, start to travel back to main huts area."* Bram looked up in wonder and immediately thought of the casualties that must have taken place. He turned around and looked at all the Pixians who stood up from the ground.

"The war's over, I got the message." Exclaimed Bram.

"How are they, how many of them are going to make it back?" asked a lady Pixian.

"I do not know that yet!" answered Bram.

Meanwhile, Velda walked through the crowd and made it to the front, Bram exchanged looks with her and nodded his head.

"We all shall move back to main huts area now" said Bram, who then walked up ahead to the combatants and signalled them to start moving back towards the main huts area. The combatants went into a formation around other Pixians and started to proceed further to the main huts area. Velda held her belly tight and led the female Centaurs by forming a line among other Pixians.

The attack team had returned back to the Kingdom of Dumberry from Mt. Pyrus including Ebbe and other final trainees who entered through the gates and reached where Soren was waiting for them. He could see the entourage returning from a distance, but could see and determine that some were missing.

He looked at them and realised pretty soon that one person was missing. Ebbe; leading the entourage; headed towards Soren with a little shame in his eyes and presented the sword to Soren by looking down and extending his arms to Soren. Other final trainees also joined him and kneeled before Soren.

" I sense someone's absence" exclaimed Soren looking at them.

Ebbe's eyes reddened due to anger as he lifted his head and looked at Soren while kneeling down.

"We have a traitor Chieftain", replied Ebbe. The other final trainees also did the same.

"The trainee with long hairs, If I am not wrong?" said Soren.

Ebbe and other trainees stood and put their arms behind their backs.

"He joined their side the moment he saw a fairy chieftain" said one of the trainees.

Meanwhile, the guards present there in the back got startled as they sensed King Ulrik's arrival. King Ulrik walked through the passage corridor and straight to where Soren and others were standing.

"The minotaurs were retrieved, we got a message from Doom," said King Ulrik.

"Also, there is a lookout for a trainee who turned joined the enemies." Continued King Ulrik. He stepped down the stairs and came near Ebbe.

"What is it?" asked King Ulrik looking into Ebbe's eyes.

"I shall present his head in your feet and his lifeless body to Lord fulcrum, my lord. I shall kill him, I will kill him." Replied Ebbe looking resolute with intense and red eyes, as he talked.

"Very well, you are a rare malison." Said King Ulrik lifting his head.

Ebbe smiled a little and said, "I am a rare malison but an extraordinary citizen of Dumberry."

"Very well, Young man, very well." Said King Ulrik as he turned back to face Soren.

"Take care of elimination of other chosen ones." King Ulrik whispered into Soren's ears who nodded in response. King Ulrik wavered his robe and then walked up the stairs with the royal guards.

"Return to your dorms, you all proved your worth and loyalty towards the kingdom of Doom." said Soren.

The sky had turned pink over Solvia where the Solvians were doing their odd daily jobs. Arlan was sitting over on a boulder near the edge looking at Pixie Forest. He sensed and heard the squealing and snorting from his side, after turning around he saw Nallbo running towards him. Swiftly, he jumped off the boulder and ran towards Nallbo to hold him.

"What are you not in the stable Nallbo" Arlan said while patting Nallbo's back, suddenly his eyes caught a leaf stuck in on Nallbo's back hairs. He got hold of it and unwrapped it.

"I will need Nallbo, Arlan, wait for my message again. Eve." Was written on the leaf. Arlan startled looked around as to know where the it landed on Nallbo's back. Then with a whiff of a wind, a hawk flew pass him and with large wings looking straight into Arlan's eyes. The hawk then took his flight towards Pixie Forest.

Arlan looked looked Pixie Forest with deep resounding eyes as his eagerness increased tantamount. Nallbo squealed again, Arlan patted and caressed his back hairs while the sun finally set.

Mt. Pyrus had been so silent after a long time, as the fairies were scared to get out of their nests and the trees near the waterfall were still recovering from the attack.

"I had got him" said one tree.

"Yes, we all saw that, how you were ripped apart." Replied another.

"QUIET, you two, let the boy think." Said a tree among them. The luminescent bands glowed while the branches stretched out towards Eve, who was still standing at the edge of the mountain looking at the Doom castle.

"Heirs of Sophie...." he uttered.

"Where shall I find them?" asked Eve.

"To the farthest seas known to mankind, you shall find them, where the range of Islands are." Replied one tree.

Eve released his clenched fist and looked slightly at the trees, then looked at Doom castle again and closed his eyes.

END OF BOOK ONE